Abishag's Story

VERONAH KISATO

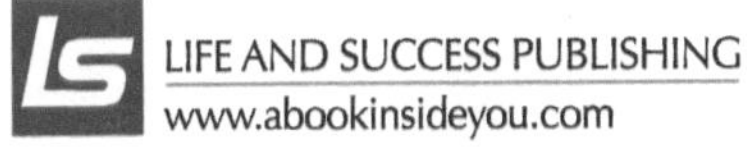

LIFE AND SUCCESS PUBLISHING
www.abookinsideyou.com

Life and Success Media Ltd

e-mail: info@abookinsideyou.com

www.abookinsideyou.com

Cover Design: miadesign.com

ISBN: 978-1-7398859-2-2

Contents

Contents

Contents

ABISHAG'S STORY

Preface

The journey on the 140 bus from Harrow Bus Station to Hillingdon takes approximately an hour on a good day. The long journey can be tiring and boring and one has to find ways to entertain oneself. There are no direct trains from my home to Hillingdon and I am a student, so taxis are not an option. Why not drive yourself there? I hear you ask... Well, I cannot afford a car: I am a single mother with a child in a private boarding school somewhere in Africa, so do the maths. I had to endure the bus ride every Monday to Thursday for half a year to get to my work placement which was part of the requirement for me to become a social worker. It was a journey filled with fun, anxiety, annoyance and everything else you would expect when using public transport. I was obviously too broke to afford a car and to put it in a better light,

I told myself, "Why should I drive when I can pay less for someone else to drive me?" Anyone who has no money might tell themselves this, so as to excuse the use of public transport. Whenever I was urged to make sacrifices so that I could afford a car, I would just ask why I should buy a cow when I could get milk from the shop.

A few weeks into making this regular journey, I noticed a good-looking lady who sat in the same spot every day. She always had headphones on and seemed oblivious to her surroundings and would alight at the same stop every time. What aroused my curiosity about this particular lady was that she was not the usual public transport type. There was an air of sophistication about her, coupled with a down-to-earth feeling, and the sort of looks that are universally accepted as beautiful. The kind of woman who, when she got on to the bus, would be noticed by anyone who was paying attention. I was so captivated by her beauty, I had to "lazima ningecheza kama mimi" (play like myself) to get her attention. I have always been a curious person, I like to hear people's stories, their journey through life. I guess I could call myself a people watcher. I finally plucked up the courage to speak with her and oh my! She was pleasant to chat with though I missed most of what she was saying – I was too busy staring. She could hold a decent conversation and the more she spoke, the more my curiosity was aroused. Let me give you a run down on what happened afterwards, during the six months that I made that bus journey. Her name was Abishag.

Chapter 1

Abishag was a very beautiful lady, her skin smoother than a baby's bottom, with no imperfections. Her big brown eyes with their long eyelashes could only be compared to those of a Friesian, a cow known for its beauty and fecundity. Her smile was gentle and when she smiled, she exposed her diastema, a true mark of African beauty. She stood tall at five feet seven inches, with size seven feet. She had long shapely legs that could put a Taita woman to shame. Her broad childbearing hips accentuated her wasp-like waist and her hair was naturally silky and very long. In short, if I looked anything like her I would have beaten Amal Alamuddin to marry the man who was then the most eligible bachelor on earth, George Clooney. She had a body to die for, which only emphasised her inherent natural fecundity. Young, old, single and married men back in her village could only dream of having her. She possessed the sort of beauty that would make any warm-blooded heterosexual man weak and speechless. Rumour had it that the chief had been in talks with her father to express his interest in paying a commitment fee: in other words a dowry down-payment. It was a sign of his intent to introduce her to his son who was abroad for further studies. In short, Abishag had beauty that could have caught King Solomon's eye like the Shulammite woman.

Abishag was also a God-fearing lady who went religiously to church although she was very shy about serving in the church. When there was a Mothers' Guild meeting in their house, she was the one welcoming the guests, and cooking too. Besides her beauty, she was the sharpest knife in the drawer and a top performer in her academic work. She had passed her KCSE/GCSE and was offered a place at the Main campus of the University of Nairobi to study for a BSc in Architecture. She had lived a very sheltered life in the village, so she decided to learn as much as she could while oncampus, to let her hair down, dust off the village mentality and embrace the unforgiving city life. Her parents were large scale cash crop farmers, so she did not want for anything that money could buy. She had her own problems, but they did not include cashflow. On freshers' night, she decided to go to the disco.

For those who have never attended a public institution of tertiary education, let me introduce you to the freshers' night. It is basically supposed to be a welcome party for the newbies, in this case, first years. I can assure you that, back then, you needed to be one of the boys to fit in.

The ratio of boys to girls so many years ago was 6:1, so the place was oozing testosterone. Girls nowadays are brave so I think the ratio has changed of late. That used to be the hunting ground for the boys or, as they would want to be called, men. They would prowl around the dance floor looking for the weakest prey in the herd. Predators do not always play fair, they choose their victims based on naivety, lack of exposure, ignorance, misfortune, age, intellect, or "leglessness", and at those parties the alcohol flowed freely. The students had just received their bursaries/HELB/Student Finance payments and so on, and they felt "loaded" and on top of the world. For the older students, especially the male species, it was a chance to pounce on unsuspecting freshers. Anyway, you get the gist.

ABISHAG'S STORY

Chapter 2

There she was, Abishag, fresh from the village, straight into the arms of the sharks in the city. Anyway, the music was blaring, the beats were pounding, the girls and boys were wiggling their waists provocatively, bumping and grinding to ragamuffin sounds and Lingala so vigorously that one might divine that they were trying to attract their future mating partners. In the same way that dogs release pheromones to attract a mate, so these guys performed these suggestive dances. As is to be expected when there is too much testosterone in a confined space, a fight broke out, and caught right in the middle was Abishag, who was with a group of other girls. She let out a loud scream as she was the only sober one: her friends were already intoxicated. Out of the blue, a tall, well-built gent came to rescue her. He seemed to command some sort of respect from the other men. He offered to take her and her friends back to their hostels. It was a relief to the young girls and they were very grateful to this seemingly very friendly man, a gentle giant who was, surprisingly, sober.

Growing up reading Disney books like "The Princess and the Frog", "Cinderella", "Sleeping Beauty", "Rapunzel" and so on, gives small girls ideas of what their man will supposedly look like in the future. All girls have dreams, whether they are in some remote village in Saudi Arabia or in California. In addition, they are bombarded with set books in Literature such as "Romeo and Juliet", "Things Fall Apart" and "The Concubine" and I am not sure what they are supposed to learn from any of them.

If you were, like me, a hopeless romantic, you went on to read every "Mills and Boon" title, as well as others, such as "The Ring" (I would not advise any church girl to read it). Some I cannot mention here because they did not have covers in those days. We were only given chapters to read in class during evening prep. After reading them we would patch them back together for them to be transported back to the schools they came from. In these books there was always a Prince Charming who would sweep a lady off her feet and take her to oblivion. Some girls expected this would happen to them in real life. Abishag was one of those ladies who subscribed to that line of thought.

When she was taken to the hostel by this gentle giant, Abishag thought her Christmas had come early and the good Lord had answered the prayers that she was yet to pray. "Haki ya mama" (swear on my mother), the gentle giant now knew where she resided and the colour of her bedding. He said goodnight and told her his name, "Ombogo" or Ondiegi in Luo language. I am not saying that he was Luo or Luhya, he just had that name. She later found out that Ombogo was a fourth year student at the university and that he was taking Mechanical Engineering – Plant Option. Rumour had it that the course was arguably harder than medicine, I stand corrected on that one. Besides that, he was in the university's rugby team and played the "fly-half" position.

For those who don't understand rugby, a fly-half is like the striker in football, or the quarterback in American or Canadian football. I use rugby because it is the only sport I pretend to understand. I am a typical girl who appreciates good things when she sees them. Who wouldn't like to see fit, intelligent boys in tight shorts and shirts that leave nothing to the imagination chase after a shapeless ball? They say rugby is the game that separates the boys from the men. I am not so clueless though, I know a try and a conversion when I see one.

On this occasion, Abishag had landed herself a try and converted it. Her heart was doing some serious cartwheels. She could not sleep that night, she hoped and prayed that he would remember her name in the morning and that he was single. I think on campus everyone is single (or is that just my assumption?), apart from mature students. It was a very strange feeling for Abishag, because she had never dreamt of taking a shine to anyone. She thought she was too principled and that she was in control of her emotions and feelings, but this was not the case this time round and all her moral faculties were in check. Love is very strange, it is not a respecter of persons and yes, love at first sight exists. There are those people you would risk it all for.

I know there is no man who can forget a woman's name if he has spent more than ten minutes with her. He can try to blame the alcohol when he forgets, or admit that, truth be told, he was never interested in the first place. They also never forget a girl's house, it doesn't matter how dodgy the place is to get to, or how dark the outside was, they will remember. Girls, now you know if he asks again for directions to your house. This was back in a time when no-one had a mobile phone, so gentlemen had to be sure tohave a good memory to remember your hostel number in the three or five storey building.

ABISHAG'S STORY

Chapter 3

The following day, Abishag woke up very tired, hoping that she was not dreaming that she had been escorted back to her hostel by an eligible bachelor the previous night. As she hit the shower, she planned what to wear for the day in case she ran into him again. She decided to break her weekly routine and did not go to shop as she usually did on Saturdays, just in case he came to her hostel and did not find her. The only trip she would be making that day was a trip to the mess or dining hall, as back in those days, food was served in the dining halls and students did not have to cook for themselves in their hostels. This was a calculated move on her part, as it increased her chances of meeting the mysterious man in this big university. So much was going on in her head, she hadn't realised what an effect one human being could have on another. All these feelings were foreign to her, not that she was complaining though. The adrenalin rush was exhilarating.

Although she was just going to the usual dining hall with her friends, Abishag dressed to the nines for breakfast, just in case. Unfortunately, Lady Luck was not on her side that morning and she did not bump into to him as she had hoped. She felt as if the clock was ticking for her. Let me tell you the reason, because most of us can relate to it I am sure. As a lady, when one meets someone, the second meeting will determine where the relationship will go. Let's fast forward to this day and age. You meet a man and you exchange contacts, then you give it 48 hours. If he contacts you within the first two hours, he is too keen, not a keeper; within 12 hours, that's a good sign; after 24 hours, you just friend-zone the person, as they are not that interested. Do not ask me who set this rule because I do not know. Don't let me get started with the WhatsApp calls because they are annoying.

Back to my story. Abishag stayed in her room hoping and praying that he would show up. The anticipation was killing her, although the scientists say it is good for the production of dopamine. She tried doing some pastime activities, but these would not get her mind off the idea of laying eyes on him again. There was no way she could concentrate on anything. She stayed in her room all day until evening. She had given up and started to prepare herself for dinner at the hall, when she heard a gentle knock on the door. She reluctantly opened it, and guess who was there! You know that feeling you get when your heart skips a beat and your knees turn into jelly that cannot bear weight anymore? That was Abishag's experience. Her legs were unable to support her when she saw who was standing there, and the door came in handy as reinforcement. There he was, the man from last night, all fresh faced and clean shaven – absolutely captivating maybe even an improvement on what she had seen the previous day. Sometimes what you see at night is not the same thing you see the morning after, if you know what I mean. He asked if he could come in, but for a while she just stared at him. After a few moments, she realised what she was doing. She apologised and let him in and he sat on the visitor's chair. Abishag was dumbfounded, she continued to stare at him, she was not sure what he was saying but she could see his mouth move. He smelt nice, which is very important, just to throw that in.

Ombogo was his name, she discovered as he introduced himself formally. He asked if he could take her for dinner as Ugali (corn meal), cabbage and beef were on the menu for that day. We all know that cabbage makes girls dull. It only makes sense when you are older and faced with the possibility of vaginal dryness and other age related issues that come with the menopause. When you are a young girl, cabbages are not the best vegetables, but once you hit your fifties, they become your loyal friend. When you get older, you eat them raw, pretending you are eating salad, but we all know their "nutritional" value. If you don't know, ask your friends. Abishag could not dream of saying no, but asked if she could change her clothes because the man was smartly dressed. Being a gentleman, he said she looked good just the way she was, but if she felt the need to change, it was fine by him. Off they went for dinner.

At dinner, he seemed to have rehearsed a set of questions to tactfully ask Abishag. She answered all his questions as honestly as she possibly could. By the end of the date, he knew all he wanted to know about her. Abishag was so besotted with him that she, on the other hand, did not ask any questions. When he asked her if she wanted to know anything about him, all she could ask was where his parents lived. He said they lived in a village somewhere, but he stayed in the city of Nairobi because during the holidays he worked for some company part time. He said he did not have very many friends because he was busy and liked to keep to himself. The dinner was okay and afterwards he took her back to her student hostel. He said goodnight and left because he had a project he was working on.

Chapter 4

Being naive is not a child-like innocence, it is a lack of knowledge about things. Sometimes street knowledge is as important as book knowledge and it is more important when it comes to identifying red flags that will save one a lot of heartbreak. Let me not spoil a good story, but sometimes people choose to ignore evidence that has been researched and proven. Naive people are just inexperienced about how the world works. If you are socially awkward, it doesn't mean that you are naive. Naive people have generally spent too much time on their own, or lived a sheltered life such that they do not know many of the things that most people take for granted. Anyway, back to Abishag.

Abishag and Ombogo saw each other every day, as he would make every effort to escort her from the hostel to her lecture halls. Every evening he would walk with her to the dining hall and back to the hostel and leave her neatly tucked in bed. On the days he had rugby training sessions, Abishag would be on the side watching and learning, or she would carry a book to read while she waited for him. She later joined the hockey club which had the same training days as the rugby club, on adjacent pitches. Abishag no longer had time for her friends. The only time she saw them was when she was going to her Sunday morning service. Ombogo was not really a church person, but he identified as one, which was good enough for Abishag. At least he believed in a higher being because she found it very difficult to conceptualise atheism. So far, Ombogo was ticking all the right boxes. On the first date Abishag had told him that she was not very knowledgeable about adult relationships and only knew what she had read in books. Ombogo was happy to wait; remember, he had other projects he was working on, so he was a busy man.

Ombogo finally completed his studies, graduated top in his class and was head-hunted for a job in a good oil company. This was a very good thing and Abishag was very happy for him. She, on the other hand, was struggling with her education. It was so hard for her to be in love and study at the same time. When she was in her lectures all she did was think about when the lecture would end so that she could see him. On the other hand, when Ombogo had finished university, he had a good job and got himself a nice flat in a leafy suburb. At this point it was very difficult for them to meet on a regular basis, so Ombogo suggested that they move in together so that she could commute to and from the university. It made sense anyway as it was close to the university, she would see him every day and she would have him to herself. It also meant that they would only pay one rent, in other words it would be a win-win situation. So they moved in together.

Life together was like a honeymoon, the sort of life people dream of, out of this world. When it came to Ombogo loving her, it was just the way she had read in the books. He responded to her needs and was a gentle and generous lover. She felt like she had seen heaven, touched cloud nine and she was now invincible. She loved that he understood his assignment like a pastor on a Sunday morning and followed the correct order of service. He started with worship, praise and worship, and when they were both in the spirit, the sermon was delivered and they ended it with thanksgiving.

There is nothing as upsetting as being with someone imagines that they know what you want, but who is not your twin. Some people are just such pompous and selfish lovers that they are just annoying. Just because something worked on someone else, it doesn't mean it will work on this one. There is no "one size fits all" in the world of love making, hahaha, not that I am an expert! At least get to know someone and their needs, people are individuals and should be treated as such. Abishag was happy, she had what most of her friends could only dream of. She forgot he had family and friends: who needs them when you have the full package eh?!

Chapter 5

Abishag was so happy that she forgot about the rest of the world and concentrated on her relationship. She gave it her all and followed her mother's example by going straight home from university to prepare dinner for herself and her husband. Everything would be ready for him when he came back home after a long day. On arrival, she would welcome him home, take his shoes off, prepare a bath for him, make sure he was well fed, then ask him how his day had been. She did all these things in addition to her "cohabiting duties", because they were still not married. If he hasn't taken you to the altar or the registrar my friend, you are not married. You have to be a fighter to prove otherwise when push comes to shove. Abishag was very loyal, she did everything Ombogo asked, from how to dress, and who not to talk to, and everything seemed perfect.

One day Abishag's best friend invited her to see a new movie that everyone was talking about going to see. Abishag agreed to go and watch it with her friends and felt that it would give her time to catch up, for it had been a long time since she had talked with them. After lectures that evening, Abishag went to the movies. It ended at around 10pm and Abishag took a cab home.

When she opened the door, she found that Ombogo had already cooked dinner and set the table and was waiting for her. He took one look at her and asked where she had been, she said that she had been to the movies with Mary. He landed a fierce slap on Abishag's face, the kind of slap that would make you forget your own name let alone your mother's maiden name. He told her never to make him worry about her like that again, then he ran a bath for her, warmed the food and apologised for having done that to her. "See what you made me do because I was so worried about you?" he said. They had dinner and made up. The following day he bought Abishag a mobile phone, one of the new Motorola ones and told her to call him if she was not home as usual.

Things seemed to have returned to normal and then, lo and behold! It had been two months since Abishag had seen her monthlies. She was not feeling too well, but she kept on taking paracetamol thinking it was just the pressure of being a student. She went to the university doctor and was given the good news that she was expecting. I call it good news because children are good. If it was up to me, I would have ten of them. They keep you in check and you move from the fast lane to the slow lane. Anyway, Abishag did not know how to take the news. She had never considered having a baby at the age of 21 with a man she was not married to. She was confused, but she thought that because Ombogo seemed so supportive, this would strengthen their relationship. So that evening she went home and prepared his favourite dish and after dinner, before they went to sleep, she announced her good news.

Ombogo looked at her with eyes that said more than words can explain. The first question he asked her was, "Have you never heard of birth control pills? How could you be so careless?" he went on, "I was not ready to be a father, I haven't built a career yet, and you are still at uni." He told her that he did everything for her and the only responsibility she had was to take care of herself, and she hadn't managed that one small thing. Later he apologised and said it was only the shock of it, he hadn't expected it to happen so soon. She forgave him and continued with life as usual.

Let me go back to my books we will continue tomorrow.

ABISHAG'S STORY

Chapter 6

Abishag's pregnancy was not the easiest ever. She suffered from very bad morning sickness and became very weak and dehydrated, to the point that she had to be admitted into hospital. Upon discharge, she could not manage to attend the university because her course was too demanding while she was in this condition, So she decided to ask for study leave and stay at home. I am not sure if this was the right move on her part. She felt sleepy the whole time and she was too tired to do any housework. As an only child, she was not able to seek help from a brother or sister, and she was too embarrassed to call her mother because she had not told her she was living with a man, let alone told her that she was expecting.

This was the beginning of her problems. Ombogo came home one day and found her sleeping. She had not cleaned the house or cooked any dinner because the smell of onions or any spices upset her stomach so that she would be cooking and feeling nauseated at the same time. She had so little energy, the house was messy and the clothes had not been washed. Ombogo was not amused, and coming into the bedroom, he roughly woke Abishag up. She jumped out of bed and apologised for not being able to do anything because of how she was feeling. That was not a good move, as Ombogo started shaking her violently, asking her what sort of woman she was. He listed for her all the women he had known who had been pregnant and had worked until the last day. He compared her to their neighbour who woke up at four in the morning to make breakfast for her husband before he went to work, and who also did the laundry for the other children and took them to school. Abishag was scared, confused, crying, asking him to stop. He instead gave her a severe beating.

That night Abishag took painkillers and went to cook for her man. She prepared his bath and he ate the food and went to bed. But instead of sleeping in peace, Ombogo lectured the poor girl the whole night about what sort of wife she should be. It was her fault getting herself pregnant in the first place. If she wanted to stay as his wife, she needed to pull her socks up and stop being lazy. He said that, women had been carrying babies since the beginning of time and it's not like it's a new thing, she was just being lazy, and it had to stop. He talked about how she had been spoilt by her parents, being the only child and having people running around after her. He wanted to show her how tough life was when you weren't being pampered. Life was tough, so should she be. Abishag cried her eyes out, but Ombogo didn't mind her. In the early hours of the morning he finally slept, but Abishag was too tired to sleep she was wondering where she had gone wrong.

The following day, Abishag asked if she could get a domestic assistant to help her out in the house. She was asked who was going to pay for it, since she wasn't working. In those days there was no "mama osha", the ladies you can call and pay to help out for the day. Ombogo finally said he would contact his younger sister who had just finished high school, and ask her to stay with them and help Abishag. This little girl showed Abishag what pure evil can be. She did not help one iota. She would wake up, talk rudely to Abishag and go away, only to come back in the evening to eat and sleep. When Abishag tried to tell her man what was happening, she was asked if she was competing with a small girl. If she was not able to cope with a young girl, how could she run a home and manage a family? She was asked again what type of wife she would be.

Abishag was confused, she had so many questions that no one could answer.

Chapter 7

woman makes a home, this is what Abishag had known all her life. She continued persevering in her relationship and it did not matter how bad it became, she simply held on to it. However, one day she decided to confide in a friend about what was going on. Her friend said that maybe it was her attitude towards marriage, if she only changed her attitude and embraced it, with all its troubles, it would be fine. She went on to tell her that marriage was not a bed of roses, there were good and bad times. Everyone goes through it and it settles after a time. Abishag decided to talk to Ombogo and ask if they could go for counselling, but Ombogo was quick to say that if she couldn't handle her own affairs, how could a stranger help her? Abishag decided to let go and survive, after all, every relationship had issues. She had been brought up in a "proper" home with a mum and dad so she didn't know any other way it could be. She wanted the best for her child. She knew that a child needed both the mum and dad to be there in order to thrive and that it was not good for the child when the parents were at each others' throats. She could certainly not entertain the thought of being a single mum.

One day Ombogo came back home and was in a very good mood. He asked Abishag to dress up, he was taking her out for dinner. It was Abishag's 22nd birthday, so Ombogo had decided to take her out, no expense spared. As they went down the stairs, Ombogo said that he had a surprise for her, and when she looked outside the door, it was a small, stylish, nice Toyota which he told her was hers, he said she needed to go for driving lessons. Abishag was reallyhappy and thought that her relationship had finally taken the right turn. They went out and had dinner and while they were there, a lady came to their table and started chatting with Ombogo. She was introduced as a work colleague, so Abishag continued eating her dinner. It seemed like the lady was not in a hurry to leave the table and at one point it got really uncomfortable because she had actually started flirting with Ombogo. However, Abishag decided to assume that there was nothing going on between them and all was well. After a while, the lady left and they continued with their meal, But it was a very quiet drive home. When they arrived, the first question Ombogo asked was, "What sort of a woman are you?"

This question caught Abishag off guard, it was an out of the blue question that she could not find an answer to. He went on to tell her that she clearly assumed that just because he lived with her, he was not desired by other women. Then he asked her why she was so relaxed when another woman was obviously flirting with him. He said that a normal woman would be up in arms fighting for her man, and that she should have told the woman off and made her leave their table when the conversation started becoming uncomfortable. Abishag's reply was that she trusted him to do the right thing by her. She was told to shut up, a man needed to feel wanted, protected and needed, "haki wanawake wako na nguvu, kama hio ndio Kazi". Abishag blanked off the rest of the conversation, the only part she heard was when he held her hand so tightly that she thought he was going to break it, and said, "Now you have decided to ignore me?" Tears were rolling down her cheeks and she was in her own world at that moment. She asked God what she had done to deserve this kind of treatment. Who had she killed in her previous life that she was paying for in this current one?

A few weeks after that day, Abishag felt sick and went to the hospital where the doctor told her that her blood pressure was too high and she could not carry the baby to term because they would both die. She was told to call the baby's father because she would have the baby that day. Ombogo came and their lovely daughter arrived, but the little girl had to remain in the hospital for some time, so Abishag went to see her every day, as Ombogo was busy working. This took a great toll on Abishag and she became a shell of the beautiful girl she once was. She looked older than her age, as though she was carrying the weight of the world on her shoulders. But the child brought so much joy to her life that she could not ask for anything more. The baby went home after receiving the all clear, and she looked like a certified true copy of Ombogo.

Chapter 8

What is love? Love is one of those English words that have never been fully defined. Love has no definition and I think that is why Christians believe that God is love because he cannot be defined. Anyway, if we stay on this religious line, the Good Book says in 1 Corinthians 13:4-8, "Love is patient, kind, it does not envy, does not boast, it is not proud. It does not dishonour others, it is not self-seeking, it is not easily angered, it keeps no record of wrong. It does not delight in evil but rejoices in truth. It always protects, always trusts, always hopes and always perseveres." In the same Good Book, men are commanded to love their wives just as Christ loved the church. On the other hand, the Good Book does not say anywhere that women should love their husbands. Women are told to be submissive and good to their men. Love is about sacrifice, tolerance and all that. But where do we draw the line when it comes to being submissive or loving? I do not mean to be a critic of the Good Book because I am religious and it is only God who has kept me sane in this place.

Abishag decided that she would make the relationship work by loving her man unconditionally. She would be patient, tolerant and persevere at doing her best to make it work. When the baby came home, it changed the dynamics of their relationship. She was busy with her newborn and Ombogo was busy with work. He would come home and find that everything was in order and the baby was fine, but he made sure that Abishag did not go anywhere apart from the clinics for the baby. Abishag now looked like she was in her late thirties despite the fact that she was only 23 years old. She lost confidence in everything, she second-guessed everything she did. She had to do everything twice before she moved onto the next thing. She could not go back to university because she did not believe she was clever enough to pursue such a demanding course.

One day when she took her daughter to the last clinic, the paediatrician asked her what she did when she was not taking care of her child. She said that she had noticed that Abishag was a very intelligent lady and that she could put to use some of her knowledge in her office in town. Abishag did not believe what the lady was saying, she thought she was just making small talk to pass the time. However, when the appointment was over, the paediatrician gave her number to Abishag so that she could call her about the job when she felt ready. She said it was part time work and not at all stressful. After a few days she gathered the strength to call. It was a well-paid administrative job, managing the lady's office while she was working at the clinic. Abishag was delighted with the idea. She went to see the lady and the office, and decided to take the job after sorting out some childcare, even here she was in luck, the lady also ran a pleasant nursery, and she was offered a place there for her daughter.

She waited for Ombogo to come home in a good mood, then she told him about the job. He was sceptical as to how she was going to pull it off, was not at all supportive, and told her it was up to her if she wanted to take the job or not. Abishag started work the following week. She was very good at it, doing the lady's accounting and managing her office. She soon decided to take part-time accounting lessons and succeeded in doing these during her lunch hours because the college was not very far from her office. After a few months she had her certificate and was also helping out other nearby firms with their accounting. Before she knew it she had become very busy. She started to brighten up and look more glamorous and cute, much to the annoyance of Ombogo.

ABISHAG'S STORY

Chapter 9

One day Abishag was late home from work and called Ombogo to pick up their child from the nursery. He gladly agreed to pick up the child and took her home. Abishag came home after 10pm that day. The baby had been fed and put to bed and Ombogo was waiting. He asked her if she thought that this was the sort of time a married woman should be arriving back home. She replied that she had had to work late, but he did not believe her. He beat her, as he would beat a snake found under a child's bed. He kept asking her who she was sleeping with nowadays. He complained that she never asked for anything from him anymore, that she had now become "Miss Independent". He told her that she had changed and did not care about him anymore. He asked what she was trying to prove to him? That was the beginning of another problem.

One should not be quick to judge others because of what they do or say sometimes. Although we are responsible for our own actions after the age of ten, we are who we are because of how we have been brought up, the values that were instilled in us, what we internalised as being the norm when we were growing up. If people grew up in non-functional homes, sometimes they do not know how to have proper relationships when they grow up. By non-functional homes I do not necessarily mean single parent families (male or female), although this could be the case. I mean situations where the children have no structure or boundaries around them. If they do not have role models or a protective factor in their family, it can turn out very badly. On the other hand, some kids who are resilient can still come out okay.

Abishag had been brought up in a stable home and that is all she had known as the norm, while on the other hand Ombogo had been brought up in a chaotic home. Although he had both parents living with him, they were constantly at each others' throats and Ombogo decided that he was going to work hard and leave that home and never return to it. But remember the apple does not fall far from the tree. What we internalise as children forms an important part of our future lives. So please, if you have children, be the best you can and don't keep children living in chaos in the name of staying for the sake of the children: you are damaging the children. That is what they will think that normal families do.

ABISHAG'S STORY

Chapter 10

omen who are only told to be submissive to their husbands have taken other responsibilities to themselves that were not theirs in the first place. God knew why he divided the roles and made sure that everyone had a defined role to play in a relationship. It is not your duty as a woman to play the loving role and the submissive role at the same time. What does that leave for the man to do? I am not saying that you should not show passion or appreciation for the male figures in our midst, but let them play their role. I had an inquisitive mind from when I was young, and I still like to find answers to questions that nobody else seems to want to know the answers to. Like why is it that a woman is the one who sacrifices so much for the relationship to work? I have heard some old women say that the only relationships that work are the ones where the man loves the woman more than the woman loves the man. I don't know if that is true but let's refer to the first paragraph from the Bible quotation.

Abishag went back to work two days later and when she was asked why she was limping, she said she had fallen down the stairs and hurt herself. She returned because she had so much work to do that she felt she could not stay at home any longer. A few weeks after the incident, Abishag had been at work and afterwards she stood in the carpark, speaking with a gentleman from another office. She did not realise that Ombogo was waiting for her outside. She had seen his car in that carpark a number of times, but when she had gone down to see if it really was him, the car had disappeared. It had happened so many times that she thought she was going bonkers. When she turned around this time, she saw Ombogo's car driving off and wondered if she was still hallucinating. So she went home and asked Ombogo why he did not tell her he was around, or stop to talk to her, but just drove off. This time he did not deny that he had been there, but told her he was giving her time with her new boyfriend. Abishag tried explaining to him that he was a colleague and there was nothing happening, but before she knew it, she was tackled to the floor and she did not remember anything after that. She came round in hospital and saw her mother and father at her bedside. She thought she was dreaming. Her mum was in tears and when she woke up started praying and thanking God. Apparently, Abishag had been beaten senseless so had been brought to the hospital. It was their neighbour's husband who had insisted that Ombogo gave him her parents' number.

When she was well, she went back home with her parents and having asked for compassionate leave while she was ill, she was now able to go back to work. Whether Abishag ever got into another relationship, you will hear in good time

ABISHAG'S STORY

Chapter 11

God is a mighty God and marvellous are His works. The Good Book says that only a fool says there is no God. That is what I believe, that is who I am; and who I am influences what I do and how I do it, but I do not want to impose on anyone, so if you do not subscribe to that line of thought please disregard my preamble. The reason I say this is because His works are not our ways, and we cannot even begin to explain them. For instance, when your human body goes through a traumatic ordeal, it shuts down to protect itself from further injury. As I understand it, that is why people go into a coma, it is the body slowing down to protect itself from further pain. This is no different from emotional pain, the body goes into a psychological spasm. I am not a doctor, but this is what I gathered: when Abishag was going through her pain in the hands of Ombogo, she was operating on autopilot, she became numb. Although someone may seem responsive in that situation, they do not react to external stimuli. So, anything you see a person doing when they are in that state is an autopilot reaction. Wah! I feel like I am ready to be given a research project, lol. It did not matter how many beatings or how much abuse she received from him, she had become voluntarily analgesic. Life, therefore, went on as usual until the day she experienced the terrible beating that made her snap out of it.

After she was beaten to pulp and admitted to hospital and woke up to see her mother and father's faces, that was when reality sank in. She knew she had to take charge of her own life. You should not think that you can come out of such situations unscathed. You lie to yourself, you need help to come to terms with what happened and learn to live with the consequences, and you never forget. So next time someone lays a violent hand on someone else you know what ought to happen. They should just leave their abuser and move on. Anyway, Abishag's parents took their daughter back home and got professional help for her. She had a good professional counsellor, but she could not remember much of what had led to her being in that situation, because it was clear to her that Ombogo honestly loved her. She had lost confidence in her ability to do anything, so university was out of the equation for a long time. Instead, he started with basic accounting and business administration courses. This is not to say these courses were easy, no! But they are courses that can be tackled in small bites, so they were manageable for her, and eventually she gained enough confidence to return to university. It took years for Abishag to recover, she worked her way up the ladders in different organisations with the support of her parents and other relatives who loved her and were also supportive.

One day Abishag was called by her director and asked if she could take on extra duties because she seemed to have very good interpersonal and inter-professional skills that the organisation needed to expand its territory. Abishag did not believe her luck, she looked at the director and asked if he was sure he was asking the right candidate because they had never met face to face and she did not think anyone would ever notice her. After what she had been through, she had decided to keep her head low, do her work and just get on with life. I don't think she talked much, because her bubbly nature had been quashed. She remembered the first time Ombogo had spoken to her: she had thought she was special and look what had happened to her then. She did not want to be rude and turn down the offer because she thought she might be set up for failure by this charming young director, so she politely asked him if she could have a think about it and get back to him. Having just dropped it on her with no warning, the director was happy to let her think about it.

Abishag prayed to God for guidance and then called her mum and dad to get their opinion about what she had been asked. Her parents suggested she ask for another meeting with the director, so as to speak with him and ask exactly what the job entailed and her responsibilities. So Abishag did just that, she booked an appointment with him and thank God, in the next meeting the director was there with Abishag's line manager which was reassuring because it looked like it was genuine.

She was given a run-down of what the job was about, but she needed further training, which they would provide, because it would involve public relations with other organisations. Abishag was happy to take up the challenge, it involved a lot of travelling, which turned out to be very good for her. Time passed and she grew into her new role, enjoying the travelling and meeting people she looked up to because they had been in the business for some time. One day in Kampala, she was busy having breakfast and going through her notes before a meeting, when she heard someone from afar saying good morning. She looked up and saw it was a director she had met before in a business meeting, a stone-faced man, who had put everyone in their place in the meeting she had attended. He knew his stuff. (You know those people who don't rely on other people to do their notes for them? Yes one of those ones). She stood up and said good morning and he asked if he could join her, to which she agreed; there was no way of saying no to this tough man who could end your career before it even began.

He was really nice, he seemed to have acquired a different persona from the one in the boardroom. Now he was very polite and pleasant to speak with. He had taken an interest in Abishag's presentation, and now they analysed it together. After a while, Abishag had to excuse herself because she had a meeting to attend, and they exchanged email addresses. She didn't think too hard about it, but it had been a very stimulating conversation and it gave Abishag confidence to know that she was not as unimportant as she had thought.

He made quite an impression on her, but she did not waste too much time thinking about it. There was no way she was ever going to meet this man again, but he was the kind of guy you would want in your corner during a boxing match. Sometimes you know in your hearts of hearts that your paths will never cross again. You count your blessings for having had an audience with that person and you move on to other things.

ABISHAG'S STORY

Chapter 12

I think every girl has a timeframe for how long she gives a man to make contact after she has given him her email address or telephone number. There is that annoying man who asks for your phone to dial their number for you, or asks for your number to flash you, while you wait. I think that makes it seem like they don't trust that they will be given the right number. There are those who ask for full names and start looking at your Facebook page while you are still with them. In all these cases, my friend, you have already been friend-zoned. Now this director was a wise man, he stayed within his 48 hour time bracket. He emailed Abishag the following morning at around 9am (a reasonable time). The email was short and straight to the point. I'll paraphrase in case I give too much away and someone joins the dots. He said it was a pleasure to make her acquaintance and some work stuff, then he signed off by saying he would like to buy her dinner one day.

Abishag, on the other hand, was in her own world. Remember the autopilot, she was still in a psychological body spasm and analgesic condition. To put it plainly, she had not been in touch with her emotions for a few years since she had left Ombogo. It had not occurred to her that she was a social being and needed a social life besides her work and motherly duties. She had set herself a routine that she followed religiously until it felt like a ritual. Work, evening classes, take care of her baby at night, following the same pattern from Monday to Friday. Weekends were for her and her daughter and visiting her parents. So this email stirred an emotion in her, not romantic, but just that pleasant feeling of being taken out for dinner by someone. It brought a smile to her face, but she did not read much into it. She replied to the email in the usual way: the pleasure was all mine, and so forth. At the end she added that she would not mind the pleasure of having dinner with him. In her heart she knew the guy was being polite and nothing more would ever happen because they belonged to two different worlds, like chalk and cheese.

Days passed and she had another email from the guy, requesting for her company for dinner at 7pm on a Thursday evening at a five-star hotel. I love Thursdays, I think perhaps because I was born on a Thursday, I assume everything good happens on a Thursday.

Abishag did not know what to say, she was curious and cautious about dinners, after all, it was dinners that had led her down that dark path in the first place, and as they always say, there are no free dinners in life. But then again, what did she have to lose? She considered the facts again: this man was well respected and had a reputation to uphold, he wouldn't trick her into anything bad. Being a simple girl from a village, and only partially assimilated into the city life, Abishag had never experienced five-star dining. The hotel was a very prestigious place with the sort of menus that you would seek Google's help to understand.

Abishag remembered her aunties chatting when she was young, saying, "You will never go wrong with chicken, just order chicken, whether it comes boiled, steamed, fried, it will still be edible." The next question was, what do you wear for dinners like that? You do not want to look tatty or as if you have just come from the office and happened to stumble into the hotel. She did not have any friends to consult, so she headed to Google, her best friend. She found some ideas that would be just right, as she did not want to give a wrong impression. What was the worst that could happen? she thought. She said yes to the invite.

Abishag had never done make up, you didn't as a girl from the village. She tried but it didn't go at all well.

She washed her face and just laughed at herself, what was she trying to do? It wasn't a date, she assumed it was a semi-formal dinner, but she had selected five outfits like any normal lady does. That day she left work slightly early to go home, shower and change. For some reason, she felt excited about going out after so many years, the adrenaline rush of not knowing what to expect, the choosing of her outfit, and all the rest of it. Despite her certainty that this was not a date, that's exactly what it felt like. After getting ready, she headed off to the hotel, and arriving fashionably late, she found him waiting for her.

He was the old-fashioned sort of man who pulls out chairs and holds doors for women, and not in a chauvinistic manner. The kind I would date anytime. He had a firm but gentle handshake, and there was none of the awkwardness you sometimes get with people who go in for a hug very early on in a relationship, which I find very confusing. Abishag stuck to the chicken plan and it was fine. The conversation at dinner was easy, and Abishag began to feel that maybe this was a date after all. Some people, on a first date, subject each other to the sort of excrutiating questions that even your doctor would not ask you on your first encounter with him. "Haki" Some dates sound like job interviews, work appraisals, or financial viability tests. He was easy going and most importantly he smelt nice.

Abishag felt she had learnt something from the man and the dinner ended on a very interesting note. Before it came to parting ways, he requested her personal number so that he could keep in touch. She gave it to him and he escorted her to where she had parked and made sure she was alright before saying goodbye and going to his own car. Would there be a second date, let's find out!

ABISHAG'S STORY

Chapter 13

The dinners became a regular thing. Abishag got so used to his presence that she would wait in anticipation for his calls or text messages. There was nothing much said in the texts, just a hello or some interesting observation. No WhatsApp forwards, or pictures from his groups. Quite a gentleman.

One day, when Abishag was in her office, she received a bouquet of flowers and a note asking if she could take an extended lunch break the following day. She was happy to, because the man was easy to be around, and having checked her diary, she informed her PA that she was taking the afternoon off to look after some personal business. Abishag decided not to read too much into anything but take the day as it came. However, when she called him to confirm the time, he told her not to bring her car to work that day, as they would use his, but to bring some official ID and a change of clothes and tip her baby-sitter because she would not be going back home at the end of the day.

That night Abishag could not sleep, she tossed and turned in her bed, speculating, guessing, thinking, building castles in the air. In her head she could see herself married to this man, having a big white wedding and a son to add to her daughter, with a house at the beach, and a dog. Perfect. What more could she ask for? She had to slap herself to bring her thoughts back to reality, because in all the times they had met, there had been no hint of anything approaching that. She knew there was no way their two worlds could collide. Not in this life. How lucky could she be? With her past record, she did not dare to even dream of a happy ever after. She reminded herself that it was just an innocent overnight stay, maybe he had a job for her to do. She had just drifted off to sleep when her alarm clock went off. She woke up so tired, she felt as if she had been chewed and spat out by an elephant.

That morning she managed to force herself to go to work, thanks to some strong coffee and cold water. But having made it in, she didn't seem to do much work. She was in her own world. She kept reminding herself it was just an extended lunch, nothing to worry about, she should just go and eat and hear what he had to say, so why was her head running away from her? She tried distracting herself with work but her heart and brain were not in sync. Time is your greatest enemy when you are waiting for something. To Abishag, it felt as if someone had ordered time to slow to a crawl. She kept checking her watch and soon realised she was doing it every 15 minutes. It was the longest morning of her life. Then, at exactly 12pm, her PA called to say she had a visitor. Her heart sank at the thought that he had come to her office, she was a very private girl and did not want to let this man see her in her office without good reason. When the visitor walked into her office she was relieved, it was someone she had never seen. He told her that he was a driver and had been asked to pick her up. He reminded her to bring her passport or some other form of ID and was very polite and professional. This was killing Abishag. She asked him to wait in the car as she cleared her desk.

On their way to wherever they were going, Abishag did not ask for anything, she just went with the flow, but she soon realised that they were on their way to Wilson Airport. She was confused, but a bit excited, thinking, could this really be happening? Whatever it was, she was suddenly game. At Wilson Airport they found the guy waiting by a helicopter. He was casually dressed, but goodness gracious, wasn't he looking fresh and edible! He looked like he had just stepped out of the shower and come to the airport. Abishag just stood there and stared, in a trance, she had never seen him in anything but a suit. He caught her eye as she approached and the first thing she really heard was, "Good to see you, Abishag." Then he asked if he could take her bag and help her up into the private chopper. Well Abishag was done! In her head she had married the guy and was already expecting his child. The guy smelt good, I think you know you like someone if you can stand their smell. She was now seeing this guy in such a totally different light that she prayed and hoped he was not telepathic and could read what was going on in her head! They went into the chopper, he thanked his driver, so did Abishag, the door shut and off they went to their unknown destination. In the skies, Abishag's head was all over the place. She did not know where they were going, but at this point she was up for anything. It wasn't clear to her whether she genuinely loved the guy, or was just infatuated because of their many dinners together, but there was something about him on this day. He appeared different and he had that look, you know the look.

Finally he said, "I am sure you have so many questions to ask. So have I. I asked you for a whole afternoon and night so that we can address all the questions we have." That caught Abishag on the back foot. It brought back so many memories that she had pushed to the back of her mind. She was so uncomfortable with the thought of having to recount everything she had been through that the guy noticed and kindly told her that she didn't have to worry because it was not a job interview – it was a "get to know you" session. Anyway, they landed in Zanzibar and checked into a hotel. In different rooms, of course, but with an adjoining door which could be locked. My dad is a pastor so I have to be polite with everything I write. They went for lunch, then went to relax on the beach. Once there, he expressed his innermost feelings, what it was that was close to his heart. Eh! Yawa! There are people who were given honey at birth not milk. Let me leave it here, otherwise I will not be able to work today. We will continue tomorrow.

ABISHAG'S STORY

Chapter 14

There is something calming about the seafront that makes you let down all your inhibitions, it makes you love nature and the people around you. Being a girl born in a village in the Kenyan highlands, who then moved to London, I can assure you, I don't usually get to experience such tranquillity. Maybe that's why our friends who are at the coast or lakeside seem to be the most romantic people we know. It has nothing to do with their ability to use language to make you agree to sell your inheritance to be with them, no, it is about geography.

In my opinion, when one visits such places, one becomes immediately assimilated to such thinking until one returns to the city. So the trip to Zanzibar was doing Abishag good, she started planning how she was going to buy the latest lingerie from Woolworths in Kenya, which is, perhaps, the equivalent of Ann Summers or Intimissimi (an Italian lingerie shop).

Well, I am not sure, but I am told Woolworths has the best. In her head she had started shaving her legs and other parts to look more appealing; she had bought new clothes to accentuate her figure; she had visited the dentist to make sure her teeth were perfect; and she had invested in the best perfumes money could buy; all in the name of making sure she was perfect for her mate. Also in her head, she had visited the gynaecologist to make sure that she was functioning alright, because it had been a long time since she had paid any real attention to her body rather than her brain.

She was brought back to the reality of the beach when the guy asked her why she seemed so distant. Was she regretting coming on the trip? Abishag dragged herself back from dreamland and said that she was enjoying the peace and quiet of the seafront. They sat down on the sand and started talking. The man said he would go first, since he was the one who had ambushed her and brought her to Zanzibar. He said he had enjoyed her company since the breakfast at Kampala and had wanted to tell her so from day one, but he hadn't want to scare her off. He had been trying very hard to push it to the back of his mind but it was impossible because she had gotten under his skin. He had taken his time to tell her because he wanted to be sure that it was real, not just a passing phase. But his heart had not stopped doing backflips since he first saw her, and every time they met, the feeling was greater than the time before. Meanwhile, in his head, he had already started making space in his bedroom closet for her and begun sleeping on one side of the bed in preparation for his soulmate to join him. Abishag was lost for words. How? Why? Was it just talk? Was he serious? Do such men have a softer side to them? So who was it that she had met in the boardroom? Despite these questions her head had already married the guy and was now having their fifth child, her hands wanted to punch the air so strongly that she had to physically restrain them from doing it.

When the guy had finished showering her with praises and telling her how much he liked her, he finished by saying that it was up to her to decide and there was no pressure and that they had all the time in the world because he was going nowhere. Abishag was screaming in her head that she was ready and did not want to go anywhere without him, but this time round she engaged her brain and instead said that he had caught her by surprise and she needed time to absorb it all. He asked if she had any loose ties to someone that she might need to end, just in case. "Some men aki don't give people too much choice."In reality how do you know if people are really single out there? When you meet someone do you assume that they are single, and that you are the only one who has noticed they exist? Perhaps some people do, I don't know. Abishag said she didn't have any real ties, but would have to think about the emotional investment, because this would be an enormous change to her status quo. It's different when it's just coffee and dinner, this new offer was a lot to take in. Anyway, the guy was not expecting her to do back flips at the very thought of his confession, and to follow that deep conversation, he had organised for a spa evening before dinner. Abishag was waited on hand and foot, literally. From body scrub to body wrap, manicure to pedicure, full body massage to a full facial: you name it, she had it done. It wasn't the kind of fun he liked, so he just left her to be pampered.

Abishag, in her heart of hearts, wished this guy would just skip the dating bit and marry her already. He seemed perfect and had been well-trained by somebody. She didn't want to spoil the day by thinking negative thoughts. She enjoyed every moment, it appeared this guy had taken his time to do some research on how to wine and dine a lady. And there she was thinking men had no clue! Here was a man who was properly clued in. When she had been pampered enough, they both went into their respective rooms to change. At dinner, the guy didn't dwell on what had been said at the beach, so the conversation was easy. When it came to the food, Abishag had no clue what was on the menu and didn't have Google at her disposal, so she was bold enough to ask the guy to order. He asked what her preference was, then ordered for her, and it was perfect. Their conversation was so interesting that they lost track of time and eventually realised that they were the only ones left at the dining area, so they went upstairs to carry on and chatted about nothing in particular until 3am. At last she fell asleep on her bed, so he went to his bedroom and slept.

In the morning Abishag woke up to find that her clothes had been ironed and clean working clothes were laid out for her. This killed her, it was so perfect. He rang her on the room phone and she got ready and met him at breakfast. She was exhausted and wasn't sure if she had truly slept or just drifted in and out of dreams, but she was happy. Abishag looked gorgeous in the outfit she was given, it was exactly what she would have gone for: not too tight, or short, or flamboyant, just simple yet sophisticated. She was almost tempted to ask what the price tag was, but she bit her tongue. The guy was suited up, looking handsome and still smelling nice and that was a plus. After breakfast, they were taken to their private chopper and flew back to the harsh realities of Nairobi. Abishag was dropped at work where she was not productive at all, too busy reminiscing over what had happened, what had been said. This was a story Abishag would not tell anyone.

No-one would have believed her, they might even have taken her to a psychiatric unit to be checked out. But the truth was, it happened. Have a good day my people and God bless you all. Time to get off the bus now.

Chapter 15

I hope you had a productive day, because I didn't. Can I call you?" said the text message Abishag received from the guy the next day. Abishag just smiled and replied, "Neither did I, yes please." When he called, he said he was shocked at himself for having been distracted and unproductive for the whole day, he had just been reminiscing about their trip. He confessed that he had never in his life thought that he would be distracted by a woman, especially not at his age, as he was no longer a young, energetic man. Don't get me wrong he was fit, he could certainly give some young men a run for their money. They had an interesting conversation and then he asked what she felt about a weekend away. Abishag considered, she had her daughter, Atoti Nya Mwalo to think of. But Atoti was still in pre-school, and Abishag's aunt had a child of the same age so Atoti would spend some days with them, especially when Abishag had to go out of the country for more than two days, which was too long to leave her with the child minder. So Abishag said yes to the proposition, and they planned it for the following month. During the next few weeks, they continued meeting for dinners whenever their busy schedules allowed.

Ombogo, on the other hand, was already married. Apparently he had been seeing another girl while he was with Abishag. He wedded the girl, and they had two children in the space of three years. He had met his match this time round, she was marking him the way Wayne Rooney the striker might be marked during a Manchester United match to prevent him from scoring a goal. Ombogo had to go home on time, his phone was confiscated for snap checks the way tellers' trays are spot-checked in banks. Screaming matches and "go and cook for yourself," games were the order of the day. He would go home, roll up his sleeves and get on his hands and knees to help with the chores.

There was no extra help because she said she was on top of things as a stay-at-home mum. She would not allow another woman to live with them, neither would he allow another man to come in, so they were at an impasse. When he returned home, the neighbours would lower the volume of their TVs to hear the free entertainment streaming from their house. He was happy because that sort of situation was where he thrived. He looked older and stressed out, but he said he was happy, so we will stick to that story, that he was happy.

Three weeks before their weekend away, Abishag was told to present her passport to the travel agent to allow them to book the holiday for Thursday evening to Sunday. She booked the Friday off work: sensible people don't skive off work, they ask for a day off. She called at the travel agent and was told the destination was Abu Dhabi. The tickets were booked, visas granted and they waited for the day to arrive. When it came, Abishag was relaxed and thought, wow! If this was a dream, she didn't want to wake up. At the airport, they went to the priority section and used the lounge, heh! They were traveling first class, not business or economy.

Abishag had upgraded straight from economy to first, skipping the middle one, and in first class it was pure luxury. I don't know the details of what happens in first class, I just know it is an experience, not a journey. There were showers, you were given pyjamas, the cutlery was fine silver and the plates were fine china, not disposable ones. There was an open bar all night, but Abishag didn't drink alcohol, and there was no pressure from him to drink a "sensible drink". As someone told me once, everyone has their own vice, for some it's alcohol, but not for Abishag – each to their own. So Abishag had not relented to the pressure to drink, she still had things she didn't want to change, but never say never. It is a woman's prerogative to change her mind, you pick up vices as you go along. The guy enjoyed his Champagne and wine and whatever other drinks were on offer, but he seemed able to handle his drink, and remained in charge of his faculties.

On reaching Abu Dhabi, more surprises awaited Abishag, it was a seven-star hotel. They were waited on hand and foot, and the fun was out of this world. By the way, Abu Dhabi is overrated and commercial, just go to Dubai, it is better. Abu Dhabi is for businessmen. It seemed like this man really paid attention to what Abishag said during their conversations. He had a brilliant memory, he remembered dates and times and it sometimes seemed as if he could read Abishag's mind, but it was just that he paid so much attention to what she said in passing and pieced the clues together to make sense of it. It was perfect: whoever trained this man in how to treat a woman, should train more men, then they would understand women. They had a wonderful time, and Abishag told me that he was very good with his hands, and he could give good massages. I do not know what happened for the rest of the holiday, I will let you fill in the blanks because she didn't divulge the details to me. She didn't confirm or deny whether they shared a room or not, and I thought it was not my place to ask. On Sunday they left and went back to Kenya. Abishag was so happy and I was happy for her when she told me.

On the Monday morning she received a text wishing her a lovely week and telling her that he was going out of the country for a week to work. Abishag was missing him already. She had gotten used to him being in the country. Even though they had very busy schedules, they always tried to meet up as often as they could. Later, when Abishag was about to close her office for the day, she received a phone call. Guess who? It was Ombogo. He didn't even say hello, his first statement was, "I hear nowadays you have started selling yourself to the highest bidder. I do not want my daughter to be brought up by a prostitute, I am going to go for full custody of my daughter in court. You will never see her again. It will give you space to sell yourself properly, without the burden of having to think about where to dump my daughter." Abishag was in shock, she didn't know what to say or do.

ABISHAG'S STORY

Chapter 16

What most women don't know is that parental responsibility for a child born outside a marriage is the mother's. If they are married when the child was born, or got married later, then the father of the child has joint responsibility. With an unmarried woman, the father can only take that responsibility from her if he can prove beyond reasonable doubt that she is not a fit mother. However, he also has to prove that every measure has been put in place and resources provided and she was still not able to improve, or that she is just not engaging with the services. That is what Abishag did not understand or know, she needed someone to increase her knowledge very fast. You always need strong people around you because in our time of greatest weakness, we cannot even pray for ourselves.

Ombogo issued many unpleasant threats to Abishag, and threw around some very serious allegations that could not be substantiated. He kept hounding her with phone calls, threatening to take her to the Children's Court. Abishag was in shock: where has this man been? He was married, why would he bother with her? He had kids of his own, why was he bothering her? She thought about leaving the country and starting afresh somewhere else but that was not an option, she had a very supportive network around her now, which she was sure she would not have anywhere else. From the last time she had problems, she had learnt that you are the master of your own fate, and you have choices in life. If you don't fix things, no one will fix them for you. The next time Ombogo called, she told him to go to court and they would meet there. She told him he should stop calling her, otherwise she would sue him for harassment. Believe it or not, Ombogo went to court to seek custody of his daughter, and Abishag received a court demand for her to make her statement. She thought, "The children's lawyers can help me with the English, as mine is limited".

Abishag was in shock when she heard the allegations he had made against her, the cheek! Those allegations could have made a nun swear like a sailor. Abishag did not know where to start, she needed a proper lawyer to defend her, but she had been given three months to respond because the child was not at immediate risk of harm. Anyway, she knew a few people she had worked with or helped who might come to her rescue. She did not want to disturb her parents with this, she would fight it herself. She cancelled all her late dinners with the guy and only spoke to him every so often, because all her free time was spent looking for answers and solutions. The guy did not know what was happening, and he assumed that she had lost interest or was distracted with other things.

Six weeks later, the guy decided to pay Abishag a visit at her place of work, because he could not stand the distance between them. When he arrived at reception, he was ushered in ceremoniously, but Abishag's PA was shocked and wondered why he had come when there was no scheduled appointment. She immediately showed him into Abishag's office and she called for tea. "I love the properly brewed office tea in Kenya, sweets, now you know why I ask for tea when I come to your office, the tea is heavenly." Anyway, Abishag was in shock, she just looked at him and tears rolled down her face. The guy was confused, were things so bad that just the sight of him could make her cry? She quickly dried her tears, tea was brought in and they drank, and then he finally asked, "Is it that bad? Who died? I can't be so annoying that I make you cry, can I?" She just said, "No, don't even think that way, you are the best thing that has happened to me for a long time, I just didn't want to burden you with my problems.

The guy was shocked, he wondered why Abishag could not trust him enough to tell him her issues, but he asked if he could be of assistance, or just give a listening ear. A problem shared is a problem halved, as they say. She decided to start from the beginning, but obviously not giving him too much information, because sometimes things you confide to people come back to bite you in the future. I think the best person to confide in is your therapist. Abishag had one, so the gory details were saved for her counsellor. When the guy heard what had happened, he said to her, "So long as nobody has died, every problem has a solution." He asked Abishag if she would trust him to help her, and she agreed. The guy said "No expense will be spared to make sure that that man never sets his eyes on that baby again, legally of course." The investigation into Ombogo's life began, no stone was left unturned in that six weeks. Oh, by the way, I call him 'the guy' because I still don't have his name, Lol. I have to get off the bus now. Have a day full of confidence in yourself and never walk alone. Thanks.

Chapter 17

eaven has no rage like love to hatred turned, Nor hell a fury like a woman scorned." Spoken by Perez in Act 3, Scene 2 of The Mourning Bride (1697).

You never know how volatile an African woman can be until you ruffle her feathers. While the way to a man's heart is through his stomach, the way to a woman's nucleus is through her child. Ombogo had touched the wrong side of Abishag: angry, furious, annoyed, aggravated, vexed; all these words were not enough to describe how she felt. As some wise old people said so many years ago, there is a very fine line between love and hate and, as my physics teacher taught me, everything has a breaking point including rubber, flexible as it is. Don't even ask what I got in physics and maths, though, my teacher in forms one to four was an ex-Black Blood rugby player (Kenyatta University), a tall, sculptured and handsome man straight from campus, need I say more? I never missed class but I am not sure I understood a word he said. Abishag had had enough of Ombogo's threats, so she decided to roll up her sleeves and get into the ring, all guns blazing, whether it was a David versus Goliath, or Evander versus Tyson; Paco Rabanne oops, sorry, Floyd Mayweather versus Manny Pacquiao, she didn't care. She would die trying. With the force behind her there was no turning back.

She booked an appointment with her assigned family court lawyer, the best that money could buy. Abishag arrived nice and early for her meeting, she introduced herself and talked to the lawyer. Shockingly, he had time for her and did not just send her to his intern to gather information. Whether he was under serious instructions, I don't know. So Abishag poured out her poor soul to this man, who quietly took notes and asked questions whenever necessary.

When he had finished asking the questions, he looked at Abishag and said "Sweetheart, if this is the case you are putting together, the children's judge will ask you to go for family therapy to reconcile. Please give me something to work with, I am sworn to confidentiality, I will know what to do regarding very private matters." Well, on hearing that, Abishag opened her heart "alifungua roho". She spilt the beans about everything, including his horrible bedroom antics, about which I will not go into details here. It was very very bad, he should have been arrested a long time ago and the warden should have accidentally-on-purpose lost his files and keys. The lawyer was in shock. In his head he was just wondering who could do this to such a pretty woman and at the same time wondering at her level of naivety.

Ombogo, on the other hand, had sought the support of his friends from campus, some top ambulance chasers, who only had experience in criminal justice and not civil or family law. They had graduated top in their class, so they had their own credentials to bluster about and had assured him that they would sweep the floor with Ombogo. He was very confident about how the case was going to go, which is laughable, because before you dish out dirt about anybody, you should make sure you clean your own nose and your own backyard.

He thought that for all those years Abishag had been clueless about what he was doing. She had the inside information, but she was too besotted to accept it. Meanwhile he had forgotten that they had never married and that his parents had never liked the girl anyway, a uni drop-out was not the sort of girl they wanted for their beloved high-achieving son. She had never had the opportunity to be formally introduced to them. When she wanted to formalise their union, all he could say was, "If it ain't broke don't fix it," or "Love is in the heart, you don't need to declare it to the world," and "Anyway, I am not ready to marry." At the time these words didn't mean anything to Abishag, because she was comfortable with him coming back to her every evening. But as they say in social work, "If it is not in writing, or there is no evidence, it didn't happen". I feel sorry sometimes for cohabiting couples. Either stay apart, or marry the person already, why are you taking yourself out of the market for a trial? Are you a sample to be tested, or a product with a price? "Tujipende" (love yourself). People have lived together for years and then one day are shocked that their "partner" is marrying someone else?" I am not judging anyone, but please understand what you are getting. If it's a business partnership, cool, but for love, please, just continue buying the milk, you don't have to bring the cow to your home, it's too expensive an investment. "Don't gamble with your life, insure it instead."(If you remember that advert you are officially middle aged or old.)

So in summary, Abishag and Ombogo were not married and he had no parental rights over his daughter, he had just donated a beautiful girl to Abishag. The lawyers established this for a fact, and started finding out more about Ombogo. Ombogo was the type of frog that hopped from pond to pond, leaving behind tadpoles. He did not take any responsibility for his own actions. Maybe some people go to farms and plant seeds, but they don't expect there to be a harvest? The PI reached Ombogo's village, went to the nearest pub and got some inside information from someone who he had bought for a few drinks. She told him how Ombogo's dad was successful, but very violent towards his wife, he treated her like trash, but the woman had stuck by him. Ombogo had moved to the city after the fourth form, leaving a girl heavily pregnant, and he was never to be seen or heard from again. The girl had a beautiful son, but she was married to someone else. It was apparent that Ombogo had had a chaotic upbringing and he seemed not to have had any attachment to his parents. He had moved to the city and never looked back. To put it plainly, he did not have a strong family network.

In the city, the neighbours were not mean with information about how he lived in his house from "mama mboga" to "mama fua" the vegetable vendor and cleaning ladies. He used to take food on credit from the local grocery shop, I don't know what he was doing with his salary. The neighbours also disclosed that, his house was not a fit environment in which to bring up children, because of the constant fights and screaming. You might be shocked what your gateman or watchman knows about your life, some true, some not true, depending on who is asking. His children were very quiet and timid, they didn't talk much, all the neighbours were sorry for the children who were witnessing such things. At his office, there were rumours about the way he used to welcome the new interns, but because of his charming personality he would get away with murder. All this was dug up in a period of five weeks.

This evidence was enough to ensure that Abishag got full custody of the child without setting foot in the Children's Court. She was represented by a family case-worker, there was no need for her to sit face to face with her ex and have to re-live the horrors which Ombogo had subjected her to. Ombogo did not believe the evidence they had against him at first. He had forgotten about everything he had done and eventually he seemed shocked himself by what he had done to the poor girl.

The court agreed that the child needed stability, secure attachment to a non-violent parent, and that Abishag provided that. They also said that Ombogo had a history of not providing for his children, so there was no need to give him another child. He was also told he had a case to answer for exposing children to domestic violence. Although he wasn't violent towards them, the trauma of them witnessing it was psychologically affecting the children. He was told to seek help before he would be allowed to appeal the ruling after ten years, when the child would be around 15 years old. Abishag was pleased with the decision. Please protect children from any form of harm. They are our future.

ABISHAG'S STORY

Chapter 18

Laziness and nosiness do not go hand in hand, it requires dedication and a serious level of inquisitiveness. That was my next goal, to find out who this new man in Abishag's life was and what was he about. Everyone has a backstory, some good and some bad. By now I am too invested not to know who Omera is and what makes him tick.

Let us start from the beginning.

Nothing had prepared the nice intelligent fresh-faced boy from Siaya Kenya for life in UK. He had passed his exams with flying colours and his mother who was a local primary school teacher decided to apply for him a scholarship to study abroad. The scholarship fell through and the only thing they could not provide for the young man was accommodation, which seemed reasonable and his mother knew one of his deceased father's brother who lived in UK. She got in contact with the said uncle seemed happy for the young man who had defied all odds to pass with straight despite schooling in an underfunded village school in Siaya. The whole village was happy for this young man and they prayed that he would excel and put their village on the world map.

Those days there was the waving bay at Jomo Kenyatta International Airport (JKIA) and a whole village would escort their loved ones to the airport with mini buses, hire their village traditional dancers to sing when they arrived or departed. This young man was no different, they came from Siaya in his former school bus with all the pomp and colour and was seen off. It was his first time to fly and he was terrified and felt physically sick on the plane. He was not embarrassed to ask the beautiful hostesses for help and his charming nature who wouldn't oblige, they were very supportive of him. When the plane hit turbulence at 35000 feet above sea level, he was in shock. Nothing prepared him for that feeling, he was prepared for take off armed with chewing gum. But the turbulence was too much for this young man although his pride would not allow him to scream. He said a silent prayer requesting the man upstairs not to let him die mid air because his poor mother would not have a body to burry. He promised God to never complain again about the road from Kisumu to Siaya because it had potholes that could swallow a whole car when it rained. The ride was bumpy that there were so many children born on that road. Anyway he didn't die, the turbulent distance was over sooner that he had expected and he fell asleep.

The Next thing he remembered was a lovely voice waking him up to ask him if he would like to have some breakfast. Of course he did, a young man like him needed all the food he could get and the dinner he had in the plane was not enough. It was a soft dinner that according to him should be fed to an invalid any way he had his breakfast and prepared for landing. On landing again he was fine because he had his chewing gum to relieve the pressure in his ears. He landed safely and went straight to immigration, back then immigration rules were so relaxed he got your visa at the airport as he landed. Unlike nowadays at the airport you almost feel like telling them "it is okay I can go back home, I did not kill anyone there, neither did I demolish my old thatched house, I have somewhere to go back to".

When he got to the waiting area, the uncle was nowhere to be seen. The young man stayed optimistic that his uncle was may be working that morning and he would have picked him later. Evening came, he was hungry and tired still no one came. He went to the nearest coffee shop and bought himself some tea with a sandwich. He did not believe how much they costed because he tried converting pounds to shillings, he stopped otherwise he would starve. It was a Saturday and there was no way of contacting the university so he slept on airport benches, come midnight the cold was too much but he survived, the light coat he carried from Kenya felt like a vest with the UK weather. The following day he tried calling his uncle nothing happened he was not picking his phone and he started to panic. He started contemplating going back home and then he remembered his ticket was one way. He remembered the lovely faces of everyone who has escorted him to the airport, their prayers and he believed that God had a plan for him. He had to man up after all, he had to be a man at a young age when his father died. He was a survivor and there was no way he would let his mother and the whole village down. He had to come up with a plan because he was to report at the university on Tuesday morning ready to embark on his academic journey.

He was approached by a cleaning lady at the airport and asked him why he was spending the second night at the airport. He explained to the lady who really felt sorry for this 19 year old boy from a developing country with no one to talk to. She showed him where he could freshen up at the airport and bought him lunch. He had his lunch and he asked the lady if she knew anyone who could house him for just two weeks until he could get himself sorted. The lady offered to take him in for the two weeks while he sorted himself. So he carried his small suit case and followed the lady at night when she finished her shift. They chatted so much although their accents were quite different but they understood each other. He managed to sign himself in the university thankfully so, he didn't lose his scholarship.

ABISHAG'S STORY

Chapter 19

Life abroad is not for the faint hearted don't be deceived by the Facebook photos, life is tough and it is up to one to stand strong it is actually a man eat man jungle, you only trust yourself and God. Everyone is always looking for someone to use one way or the other, it is not always genuine especially for the immigrants and it is up to one to choose who will use them and what they will benefit from them. All physical and emotional energy is out to be tested, your level of resilience is the key that will determine whether you survive or not.

It doesn't matter if you are someone's sister or brother, you have to pay your way because life dictates so. The young man from Siaya was not lazy being a first born among seven siblings did not allow it. He was used to hard work, so after registering at university the lady who was a single lady with two children doing manual jobs he had to also chip in. In London no one will cancel their shift to show you around because people are paid by the our not all though some receive a monthly pay. So the young man was given a London map and told to do find a job and support with the bills.

He was a young energetic man with a strong back to handle a job. Those days there were many jobs it was up to you to choose especially casual labourers. He registered with an Agency and got job as a hospital porter and a night one working in a warehouse. He went to university two and a half days and the rest of the days were spent working. He was told as many of us who live in London were that you do not go abroad on holiday, you go to work and you will rest when you die. The first few days were so hard on him, he did not have time to eat or sleep, he worked back to back shifts. The only time he had to rest time was during the train and bus journeys and take away on the bus was his way. One day he told the lady that he was giving up one job, the lady looked at him and laughed. She told him the first five years abroad are the productive when he still has the organic food still flowing in your blood stream. Once he tested the genetically modified food abroad for five years, his energy levels go down and will feel it in his body, anyway no one dies of hard work. So he soldiered on, he worked so hard and sent money to his family in the village saw his siblings through school, built his mother a house, built a church and everyone was happy back home.

It is different nowadays you should be lucky to get a cleaning job as an international student you have limited time to work by 2005 students were only allowed to work 20hours a week now I think it's 10 hours a week. This is not to discourage anyone but if you are not street smart or academically blessed it is a gamble. Some are lucky some luck is never on their side, depending on which one you are.

Omera soldiered on and did his three years at university and passed by very fast.   The university people were so impressed that they offered him a scholarship to do his masters. He agreed because he is an Omera, how could he say no to an opportunity to exercise his medullary oblongota, for an Omera being able to hold a intellectually stimulating conversation is key, you have to have a suffix of MBA or MsC, Hons etc when handing over your business card. Your title means everything, being one is not a tribal affair it is a lifestyle and your credentials dictate it all. So he went in to do his masters while still holding his jobs. Having a white collar job is not a priority abroad, it is what is is your pay check worth? And the flexibility of the job. To go through University, you take up jobs that will allow you to work in a flexible way and be able to go to uni at the same time. There is nothing like pride, there is nothing like class, it is levelling ground out here, you may be the chief's son in your village but when you land at that airport, you leave your crown there and wear humility and humbleness because if you don't humble yourself willingly, this country will humble you.

Chapter 20

It will not be fair to bash life in UK without giving the positives, if it didn't have any advantages most people would have rolled up our mats and headed back to our respective villages. Life abroad opens you up for new possibilities, your mind sets are changed and you find a way of embracing diversity. Like any other big city in the world, London is a very multi-cultural city arguably the most multi-cultural city in the world. When you land in London you learn very fast that different people view things differently and that what you thought was good in your village does not mean it is good for other people.

As a typical Kenyan, Omera loved a good laugh and speaking some exceptionally good English. This does not work in London, some things you would laugh about in your village may be offensive to other people, and he had to learn to tone it down. Anyway let's stick to the getting rid of mind sets and opening yourself up to new possibilities.

Omera was lucky or blessed to complete his masters and was headhunted by a certain bank to work for them. There was a shortage of labour because it was a job that one could only dream of, he accepted the offer immediately. With the job came class, different set friends, different mind sets because it was only natural for him to change. He stopped partying at club Afrique, East London and moved from East to West London. Omera had landed on his feet and felt that he is living abroad and decided it was time to settle. His siblings were doing well, his parents and relatives were catered for, and he finally met his long lost uncle after he settled in West London. Everything was going on well for him and then one day he realised, every time he went to his local he would see these very beautiful girls hanging out.   He plucked courage, wore his charm offensive line and went to speak with them. He took a shine on the light skin one not knowing if this a case of the hunter becomes the hunted.

Let us find out.

Omera totally forgot about the girl he used to hang out with called Nyadundo because she was working double shifts from Monday to Sunday to send money home to support her son and parents. Nyadundo was lovely mother of one but their social status were no longer compatible according to him. It had now become a mismatch for him. Nyadundo was dark and did not have command the Queen's language the way the young beautiful light skin did. So Nyadundo was left never to be contacted, was blocked from all communication channels and she confirmed from her friends that his number was still working, she counted her losses and moved on.

Omera decided to pursue Nyarabuolo the Lightskin (yellow yellow). Nyarabuolo was very beautiful, she had class, sophistication, worked in the city of London and there was no known evidence of her previous dating escapades. She came with a clean slate, right age and their combined earning power they would be a firm not a family. So it only made sense for Omera to see the future with his naked eye, he calculated the risk and saw it made sense to amalgamate their social business to leverage their social rankings in society. All these seemed like a good idea, he coated her and by the end of the first year, he decided to ask her for her hand in marriage. Nyarabuolo accepted and asked him to make an honest woman out of her.

Nyarabuolo was the kind of woman who knew that she wanted to get married therefore she had planned everything beforehand and the only thing that was missing was her dream man. She set everything up a date for the dowry payment and in no time she took her annual leave and the travelled to Kenya for bride price payment. Omera was ready, he had already gathered his strong army of friends and off they went to the land of Rabuolo (Irish potatoe in Luo language). Rabuolo village women don't come cheap as you may be aware as a Kenyan man you need to have balls of steel to marry one of them and Omera was a fit candidate because he possessed them.

On the day, Omera was suited and booted to kill, his ironed suit could slice a fly into pieces as Omeras take these occasions very serious, no Omera goes to pay their bride price in something less than a suit. Beg, borrow, hire or steal, they need to make a good first impression on your parents in law. The ceremony went well and the bride price negotiations went well, the bride price at that time was one million Kenya Shillings that was equivalent to a mortgage down payment for a house in Karen (leafy suburbs of Nairobi) Omera with his strong men entourage paid the bride price as Omeras don't take embarrassment lightly, they have a reputation to uphold.

Chapter 21

Omera had embraced diversity and decided to make an honest woman out of Nyarabuolo but if you had asked him back then he would have profoundly said no to someone from that tribe because of their bitter sweet relationship but coming to London and breaking the mind sets he thought he had landed a jackpot. They wedded the following year in an elaborate ceremony. It obviously took place in Nairobi St Mary's School where who is who in Kenya schooled in those day and they were invited. The wedding was full of pomp and colour, the dancers came from far and wide to entertain the invited guests. People danced as if their lives depended on it, they drank like they were being paid as it was an open bar and it went on with no glitch.

Omera was lost in the enjoyment of leaving his lonesome face of being a bachelor and boarded the ship of matrimony. The ship sailed and there was no turning back because he had sworn for better or worse and he wanted to maintain that like a total man. He would cross river Nyando famously known for being unnavigable as one would need to brave the crocodiles for this matrimonial ship to remain afloat. In their first month of their union they decided to do everything together as a unit. They did everything jointly, had joint bank accounts and any legal document included both their names.

Nyadundo on the other hand worked hard and after a while she was seconded to do nursing at university while still working. She went to university, polished herself and became the "bees knees" as my friends from South of London would say. She secured a job as a nurse and went on to do her masters got her child from Kenya and they stayed happy. Before long she was married to some nice "Mzungu" (white man) she met at the hospital and she was fine.

Before long they were blessed with twins and Omera couldn't be happier, he was a hands on dad and worked so hard as life abroad always dictates, there was no external help and day care made no sense because the cost of it was the same as the salary the wife would get working part time and so they decided she would be a stay at home mother. Those days there were no subsidies to child care, I think nowadays the government pays part of it and there is child benefits, don't quote me because I haven't ventured there yet. Life was good with one income Omera worked hard gave his wife the mandate to run the house which was a good idea.

Omera was alright until the children went to school, every weekend there was a "Chama" informal meetings where people meet to contribute money towards a project or a course, or there was a function to attend, those things involved meeting with other couples over the weekend. I don't know where they get the energy, it is really tiring by weekend I just want to lock myself somewhere and be quiet, but that's just me. He didn't realise that in this meeting he was chauffeur, he felt like an outsider because that was not his crowd. The functions and meeting were good but he felt like an outsider due to language barrier because they spoke a Mount Kenya language and he spoke the Lakeside language. What started as funny stories got to him and he felt as though he was the one who married into the tribe and not his wife who married into his tribe. Sometimes they made negative comments about his tribe and try to qualify their words with the standard phrase "you know what we mean" to make him feel better but it didn't. His wife on the other side was a major contributor to the stories which shocked him, he didn't believe it is the same lady they shared a home. He took it in a stride like a strong man he was and let it slide.

As this went on, he decided to burry himself in drink and work. Life went on bills were paid, the children were happy, the wife was happy so life was good as they say "happy wife happy home". He missed Nyadundo because he had no one to share those funny stories and Nyadundo got him but unfortunately she was happily married to the love of her life and there was no turning back.

Chapter 22

Marriage is honourable, instituted by God at creation and hallowed by the teachings of our Lord Jesus Christ. Marriage is therefore not to be entered into lightly, but reverently, soberly and in the fear of God. Those are the words that kept resonating in Omera's head.

Had he just rushed into this relationship without thinking of the repercussions?

Why didn't he listen when everyone around him was talking about their incompatibility?

He was married yet single, they had very different views in their relationship, they did not agree on most things apart from how they raised their twins. She made no effort to learn Omeras language and he felt like an outsider in his own house. Anyway he was determined to make it work, so he decided to be mechanical and everything worked for both of them.

He was present physically, participated in the activities and provided for his family.

This decision was right for him at the time because the whole household was busy, the children had grown and were in full time education his wife had gone back to fulltime employment. The evenings were busy as they all brought work home, children had homework and so forth. The problem came with the ugali/sima, whether it was cooking, serving and eating, Nyarabuolo was not so good at preparing it the way Omera's liked it. Nyadundo used to cook serve Omera ugali in a way that it is hard to put it on paper, 'I will leave your imagination to run wild on this one' as you know Ugali making is a skill that cannot not be taught, you either have it or not.

Omera loved his Ugali well done with the smell emitting from the kitchen that would make one crave ugali all the time. Making ugali is a process, it is not the end product that matters, it is the preparation, don't use cold water, allow the water to boil properly, after boiling you add some little flour and wait for it to simmer a bit then start stirring, then you add more flour. When serving ugali for a typical Luo or Luhya man you do not serve it in a hot pot and give him a fork and knife. You serve ugali on a flat plate and please it must be a generous portion. "I always have a problem when I go out with people who are not Luo or Luhya, they order small ugali and insist on speaking on my behalf saying that one portion is more than enough, so to be polite you say okay and go top up at home". There is no need to cheat your stomach, you either eat or just drink water and sleep.

In not so many words Omera felt starved in more ways than one and felt he had everything but not fulfilled and what kept him going was the vows he made before God and his family and friends. Having been brought up by a single mother "widowed" he understood how difficult it was for him and his siblings. The social stigma that surrounded them, although people did not say it to their faces, they knew they were being frowned upon. He was determined to not let his two lovely children to go through that. To vent his frustrations, he worked harder and became an exceptional employee and was offered a managerial role in his company.

Despite the fact that he hit the bottle ever so often, it didn't affect his productivity that in social work would be seen as not a problem because you are a functioning human being but medically not acceptable to be a functioning alcoholic. This was a perfect opportunity for him to escape, he was able to afford after school private clubs for the children because he was away most of the time on duty in other towns. This worked very well for their relationship because they were not living out of each other's pockets. This went on for years until the children were all grown and went to university and then Omera was called to the CEO's office for a brief informal meeting. He did not know what was going on but he knew he had been a good boy and his nose was clean. He took very cold water to calm his nerves this face to face meeting was rare as they had been in virtual meetings with the boss but she always sent an email to seek audience with him. This time round she had called him to her office. When he got into the office, he sat down like a chicken that had been rained on and prayed that his boss had not caught on with his drinking. The boss realised how nervous he was and flashed a smile and told him to relax she just wanted to run something by him before the next board meeting as she had discussed with the company chairman who was in agreement. That sounded so positive and he sighed with relief, she went on about how that was not a formal supervision (appraisal) but an informal chat, the board liked his work and they think he is now ready to run a whole branch of the company on his own. This came as a shock because based on past experience some things just betray you when you are foreign the penny dropped when she said the position was in South Africa.

Chapter 23

They say absence makes the heart grow fonder and in the same vein they say out of sight out of mind so which is which? Do long distance relationships work if you are married? In my honest opinion, they don't but boyfriend/ girlfriend relationships can work. When someone is married it is engraved in their brain that they are in a relationship hence the need for companionship while when you are single or in a girlfriend boyfriend relationship, you know you don't have anyone so the need for companionship is at a distance and if you are abroad the chances of you getting lucky are second to none especially if you have lived there for a long time.

When you are single you find other copying mechanisms that work for you like working double shifts and sending money home, subscribing to interesting channels, whatever tickles your fancy. Other people have found other copying mechanisms that it would be not fair to put it in my book lest one start suspecting themselves of being part of Abishag's story. Anyway I stand corrected but we can argue until tomorrow but the truth stands, may I demystify the common misconceptions that single people are all over the place, you will be shocked, their lives are as boring as the person next door apart from the fact that they can up and go without thinking about anything or anyone after all his children were adults.

Omera accepted the South African appointment and was ready to move down south. He went home very excited that evening and spoke to his wife about it and she was not amused. There was no way she was leaving UK to live in Africa and it will mean that she has to start afresh and find a new job in Africa which would not be a problem and was also worried about alleged insecurity in had heard about SA. They agreed that she remains in UK with the two children while they were still at university and Omera would be visit and she would do the same. It worked perfectly for Omera as he would be alone in SA where they can cook very good organic Pap (ugali), the main word being organic. Anyway they completed all their logistics and it worked out alright for both of them. Omera punched the air and did summersaults and cat wills in his head because he knew this would give him the much needed break and he would retrace his steps in life. He felt he needed time to regroup with himself and have a good talking to himself and tough decisions had to be made.

Omera settled well down under, it was quite a culture shock for him after being in UK for a long time, he did not believe how relaxed it was in South Africa and he had a work and life balance unlike when you as an African immigrate abroad the motto becomes, 'You will sleep the day you die or you did not come to Europe for holiday'. So Omera was more productive and was very outstanding at whatever he did as he did not resort to alcohol and family issues. He was promoted to head the whole of Africa by his organisation which was quite an achievement by any standards.

On the other hand, with more money comes more responsibilities like entertaining, membership of all the exclusive clubs that who was who patron and this coms the temptation of testing South African Pap (Ugali). If my memory serves me right, I was told that South African women are taught how to prepare pap from a very young age. Their pap unlike Kenyan Ugali is made so soft that you can scoop it like ice-cream. Although Omera had sworn never to taste pap because he was used to ugali, he couldn't resist the temptation of pap. Pap unlike ugali is made in a special way, the process is very long but you will appreciate it after tasting. There was this one lady who had been daring Omera to try out her pap, and as they always say, the way to a man's heart is through his stomach, am not sure how true that is but anyway. Some people are very good cooks but are still single, as I said before, I don't understand why, Omera decided to eat pap and that was the beginning of the third chapter of his life. That is his story.

Chapter 24

"Abishag, I have booked a holiday for all of us and that includes the little Miss sunshine", these words came as a shock to Abishag as she was not ready for the family meet holiday. As a single mother she was very protective of her daughter that it did not occur to her that there will come a time when she will introduce her to anyone therefore this brought out a side of Abishag that Omera had not seen.

The honey moon phase was over and was asking questions that needed to be answered by Omera, her antennas were on high alert. She wanted to know everything about him including his blood group if this was possible. When one wants to meet someone's child that is so intimate, it's like asking to see under someone's bed although some people do not mind introducing their children to new partners but Abishag did.

Abishag understood that everyone brings baggage into a relationship, the question is do they declare their it or wait for you to discover bit by bit. At that point she started asking herself if she is able to shoulder Omera's baggage and if she had the strength. I personally believe there is someone for everyone, there are some things I cannot handle that someone else can although either way sacrifices have to be made. Abishag kept asking questions I am not sure she wanted to know answers to but the way things were going, she was besotted with Omera whether she was in love with him or the idea of being with him is a question I will needed to ask her at the time.

Omera was taken aback because it was not the response he was expecting because he thought it was obvious that one day they would one day go on holiday together as a couple. He was forgetting life is not that straight forward, some people do not leave in a world of assumptions.

So Abishag continues to ask, what had brought the idea of the holiday about, why did they have to go with her daughter as it was going to complicate her life because she had to explain to her who he was, where, why, how etc and Omera replied that he wanted them to be a family. He was determined not to lose Abishag at any cost, he would take a bullet for her at that point because in his head he had met his soulmate and he was determined to keep her no matter what it takes. The holiday with her daughter was out of question for the time being according to her it was time they had the heart to heart. Omera had to regroup with himself and tell himself it was time he came out and told Abishag about his perfect life. He asked Abishag over to his house in the leafy suburbs. Abishag was sceptical about the whole idea because she had knew better but then again she also knew that life is too short and risks have to be taken for one to grow.

When Abishag arrived at his house, she got him preparing dinner for the two of them, his culinary skills were second to none all the questions Abishag had I think flew out of the window after eating and was asked what questions she had. She just asked what about her, what was the situation between him and his ex or was she really an ex? By the way, do Luos from the lake side divorce? Am yet to hear them divorcing anyone, haven't come across a divorced Luo, they just add to their fold, I stand corrected on that one. He said, he had not yet divorced her on paper but she was not in the picture.

Abishag was shocked and the thought of being a second wife or a side chick would go against her values. She had to think about what she wanted and to make matters worse it is now legal to have more than one wife in Kenya so she was not going to use that as an excuse for not staying with him. He had not shown her anything to make her believe that he was still in contact with his wife? Was she going to throw the relationship out of the window and let someone else who can handle that arrangement come in? To quote Coolio the hip hop artist who said that "I'd be a fool to surrender, when I know I can be a contender. And if everyone's a contender, the everyone could be a winner."

Chapter 25

Abishag was aware that in life the decisions you make not only affect you but they affect everyone around you as the Swahilis say *"unashika waliomo na wasiomo"* translates as it catches those in it and those outside it. So Abishag had to weigh all her options because she knew whatever she decided to do would not only affect her but her family and the others. On the hindsight, does she have to worry or care about what anyone else thinks or says. Will people really care about what she does with her life after all did anyone care about hers when she was going through what she went through? On the other hand she had to put other people into consideration, that's where her values and beliefs came in.

She wondered why Omera had to spoil the status quo because it was working for her and she didn't have to think about it and she was fine going with the flow. On the other hand Omera was in love with her there was no question about it and wanted more. I think human beings are never satisfied, we always ask for more it doesn't matter where you are in life, you bargain for more. I am not sure one person gets hurt so Abishag knew she would not be happy if Omera decided one day to say they be just friends. He knew he had a reputation to uphold and therefore was not in a hurry to let go of what he had and embrace the new because it would only spoil the brand name they had established. Did he love her enough to bite the bullet and face the consequences, not sure he was. When you have built a brand and a name and you are seen as a pillar in society, would you lose it for love? Not for a business man.

Anyway Abishag had a lot to think about, she had also built her own little brand and she also wanted it to maintain. If she was to sacrifice he would also have to sacrifice but when two strong headed people meet, one has to backdown and for sure, it wasn't going to be her because she had sacrificed too much in life and she decided to cool off things with Omera and ask for a break. Omera was shocked but understood that she also needed time to regroup with herself to see what happens. Abishag continued with her life, they would talk on the phone with Omera as and when time permitted.

When they were on a break and Abishag was away working one morning she stepped into someone's office and she met a guy she used to go to church with back in the days. She thought those days he was alright and then they meet and she thinks the man is fine. Anyway they finished the meeting and exchanged their number as you do

One day they agreed to take time out of their busy schedules to meet up for coffee and chat in town. It was so exciting because they had a lot of catching up to do. They spoke about everything from village life to schools they went to, what happened after school and everything else. They had so much in common, the guy had gone to US to study and he never married although of course he had relationships but he was a workaholic so he was fine.

Remember the chief's son from the village, that's it. He was still available and he sort of hinted that he had searched and did not find another Abishag so he gave up and decided to enjoy his life. For those of us who take buses especially bus 83 from Golders Green to Ealing Broadway can relate to this, you stand at the bus top and the bus is due, it comes 15 minutes later, not only does one bus come, they come in pairs. You decide to board the empty one because you get a space to sit then when you are halfway, there is an announcement, 'the destination of this bus has changed, please listen for further announcements' when you listen carefully, it says it will terminate at Alperton station. Mind you the other bus that was full has already left so there is no catching it. So you end up getting late for work, and if you work in a factory, it is shift work and when you are late, you find someone who was waiting for work has already been given you space, very frustrating but what to do. Making decisions is not easy.

Chapter 26

Do we really get over our first love? There is something about first love that cannot be explained why we never get over it as much as we would all want to say we got over it a long time ago, evidence shows we don't but we have learnt to leave without them though. This cannot be compared to your first crash or your first anything else you may want to call.

First love is interesting especially if you had a good first experience with them, remember the selfless love, the kind hearted gestures, no ill intentions and remember what you get from the relationship but what you invest in. I think it has on hold on you because it is the first time you love someone outside your family unconditionally. You build memories in the hope it would last forever. Some may use this as a measuring unit for the people who come next in their life "I wouldn't advise that, not a good idea", remember you were young then, experimenting, you had no inhibitions and you were exploring new possibilities.

Your brains had no worries, you had not polluted by selfish things you want to get from the relationship, so please don't imagine the person you are with now is boring, they have other things on their mind but if you are still in your early twenties, you don't have an excuse. You still have all the energy and time to find and experience it. Anyway I was not writing today to remind you of your first love. Let us continue with Abishag's story.

One day Abishag was in her office she had a phone call from her long lost neighbour telling her that Ombogo had been involved in an accident and was in a comma. This news was devastating to hear not just only for her but anybody, anyone who has a heart. She just hanged up the phone and she just imagined if this guy died, her child would be without a father, that is not something you would wish for your worst enemy. She called the neighbour to confirm where he was and who was looking after him. He had apparently moved to another part of town so it was difficult for his wife to do the commute with the young children. After getting details she went down on her knees and prayed so hard to God, reminding God of all promises he had made to human in the bible from Genesis to

Revelation. Their life together started flashing through her mind and obviously, she was only remembering the good times they had as you do.

The problem with first love it makes you have selective amnesia, you choose to remember some things and forget others. Her next stop was the hospital that evening, it was past visiting hours but with her charming nature, she managed to charm her way in to see him because I don't think she wanted to meet her successor. She found a nurse and a doctor attending to Ombogo who looked different from what she remembered. She held his hand and whispered something in his ear and left, Abishag did not tell me what she told him. She spoke to the doctor and the doctor explained that he was in an induced comma because of some swelling in his brain after the accident but there was hope that he would get better. She asked if there was anything she could do, but was told that she needed to pray that he makes it alright but they were not sure if they will be able to walk again but it early days.

Abishag left the hospital and went home very sad and decided to fast and pray for him to get better. It is always good to know someone you dislike is still somewhere you can still talk and quarrel, it doesn't matter if you call to fight everyday but you wouldn't want anyone you know to die, it's very painful as there is a finality in death that makes you shudder at the thought of it.

Chapter 27

You may ask why Abishag would assist Ombogo after all he had put him through. It is because Abishag was born in the village she knew that you greet people where you go including public vans but in the city that's unheard of. She grew up with pastors as parents (the old kind). She always knew that once the sitting room door was opened in the morning it was not closed until night time and if it was closed there were always seats outside for people who come to the compound and seat. All these she internalised although she may have learnt new ways but the values instilled in her still stay.

Abishag knew Ombogo does not pray but needed prayers and she was not sure if the other woman or let's respect her his wife was a believer. You may not be a prayerful person but when the doctors say 'wait and see what happens'. Most people will not admit to praying but those silent words in your head wishing and hoping, rearing the person to hold on a bit more is prayer' and we all need it sometimes. So her fasting seemed a bit over the top but that was the only way she knew how as a Christian.

For the next few days she went to hospital to see him whenever she could and finally there was a sign of life, she called the nurse and they checked him and said she was right, he seemed to be coming round. They asked her to leave the room as they support him, left and continued praying while waiting, within a short time the nurse said he had woken up but quite exhausted but if she could see him for a few minutes while she goes to call his family. During the short conversation Ombogo couldn't talk much but just whispered a thank you to her and his eyes were tearing and Abishag told him that her work there was done and she was happy he was better. He looked at her and said in a distressed voice, 'please don't go' and she told him she had to leave and that his family must be on their way because the nurse had gone to call them, besides she had to go back to work and later prepare for a business trip abroad. The moment she left the first person she called was Omera and explained to him what was happening and Omera was so supportive and said he had friends at that hospital so Ombogo would be taken care of well and to be at peace on her trip. It surprised Abishag, Omera did not sound worried about her reconnection with Ombogo, he was very confident in himself or was he being corky. 'Wallahi, until you meet a self-actualised individual, you will think this is not a normal reaction 'although Omera laughed at her readiness to help others despite what they do to her and just put it down to naïveness and her upbringing. He knew she can't just sit back and fold her arms of she knew someone somewhere needed her help and she was the type to jump in and think later about how they were not supposed to be helping them. If you don't get your woman, your woman will look for someone else to confide in and we can pretend it doesn't happen but it does, everyone needs someone to confide in. Some men you wouldn't dare tell them anything, it will be held against you for the rest of your life.

ABISHAG'S STORY

Chapter 28

Despite what we want to tell people or tell ourselves, we all want that special someone in our lives in other words, we all want to love or to be loved, and including me, yes, for those who think am made of steel, am not. But this does not mean that people are weird, scared or sad for being alone.

Sometimes in life things happen and people decide to stay alone and enjoy their own company and laugh at their own jokes. It doesn't mean that they are sad and miserable, it just means that there are comfortable within themselves but a question arises when it comes down to who and why. We might have so many things in common but when it comes to the spark; that is a must, some may call it chemistry. One might be the lothario of their time but may still be struggling to find the one because of the spark. That's for dating, for marriage am told people marry for different reasons and they marry 'marriage material', am yet to find out what that means, but I can research and let you know.

When Abishag was away, she did not bother calling the hospital to find out how Ombogo was doing because she trusted Omera to do as he promised as he promised to get him the best doctors he could find for him to get well. When she came back she called Omera to ask how things were and was told he was getting well and they think he will need some physiotherapy when he gets out of hospital although he would spend quite sometime in the hospital. So Abishag knew he was okay so there was no need for her to see him after all her work there was done, she thanked Omera and offered to buy dinner of which he agreed. It's not every day a man 'in Africa' is bought for dinner by a woman.

The dinner date was on a Thursday and not a Saturday 'am not going to elaborate on this one' I will let you fill in the blank and it went well, there was lots of catching up to do but they did not address the pink elephant in the room. Abishag was praying that Omera doesn't bring the subject of moving in together again and her prayers were answered, he did not mention it instead they talked about Omera's progress. He asked her what she was doing over the weekend she said she was going out with a friend for dinner. He tried to push his luck by requesting a meeting after the dinner,

Abishag declined therefore Omera did not insist, he was going to play golf anyway and he would stay at the club till late anyway.

ABISHAG'S STORY

Chapter 29

My life is my own business and how I choose to live it is my problem and not anybody's business, that is what Abishag was dreaming at night in her dreams not knowing that that is a cliché. In her heart of hearts she knew that her life was not hers, she had a child to think about, her parents, her work so she couldn't behave anyhow and she did everything she could to protect that. That was what was so challenging and complex for her because she didn't know her life had become someone else's business. Once you decide to get involved with anyone then your life becomes their business either directly or indirectly, and it will be very heartless of you to just do things that affect other people and leave them to pick up the pieces when it all goes pear shaped. So when Abishag had gone on her business trip Ombogo had received an unexpected visit from a "friendly good Samaritan with a good heart".

Abishag had given all the details to Omera about the hospital Ombogo was admitted and asked him if he could get him a good specialist doctor to attend to him of which Omera obliged. This was a perfect opportunity for Omera to finally put an end to all these shenanigans of Abishag caring about her ex enough to visit him in hospital after what he had done to her. He suspected that the visit had opened some healed wounds for her to start dealing with again and that's why she had gone to this unexpected business trip to get away. Omera wanted her Abishag back in one piece with no broken hearts or anything to mend. He was madly in love with her and he couldn't bear the thought of not having a whole her, he had sworn to himself it was either all or nothing as far as she was in the picture. He had to have her for himself, mind, body and soul whatever it took, he would take a bullet for her, crawl through hot coal on his bare belly or walk on his knees. The whole time she was away he couldn't bear the thought of being far from her, she had grown on him as for this woman he could give his right arm.

Apparently, during the hospital visit, Omera had spoken to the consultant who apparently belonged to his 'big boys club, or the Americans would love to call it, his fraternity. They had spoken at length about his condition but obviously not intimate details because of confidentiality clause in his place of work of which Omera respected. But they had given him the best help they could to make sure he was well enough to face him after, you know even when one is going to be interrogated, they have to make sure that they are in a fit mental state to handle the interrogation in case they put a strain to their heart because no one wants blood on their hands. They had a reputation to protect and so much to lose for what exactly but knowing Omera he would have put anything on the line to have this woman.

So when he was sure Ombogo was well enough to hear what he had to say he paid him a visit. Ombogo was shocked to be paid a visit by this friendly stranger who was very down to earth but looked like he was not struggling in the financial department. He was very confident in himself but not in a pompous way. He pulled a chair besides him and asked him how he was doing and if he was being taken care of properly. He said he was assuming may be he was the director of the hospital or someone of influence, he was thinking that the prayer of repentance he had offered to God had been heard and answered very fast.

Ombogo's stay at the hospital was like he was paying for extra private services at the hospital. He had been waited on hand and foot and he had visits from doctors and consultants every day he thought it was by shear luck not knowing he was sailing in someone's else blessing. This reminds me of people who walk around thinking they are favoured and that God visited them without sending anyone 'translate that to your mother tongue and laugh with me, 'wanadhania Mungu amewatembelea bila kutumana'. My friend you are receiving those favours because someone put in a good word for you or someone somewhere is praying for you and you are busy insulting others, may God forgive you my friend. Climb down from your high horse and look back in your life you didn't do anything to deserve unmerited favour, anyway let me not get too personal.

So Ombogo was deluded that he was that important for people to treat him that well. Anyway, he was in for a rude shock, when Omera heard his stories and his grievances and empathised with him he dropped the bombshell. He just told him that he was happy he was well and he should be thanking Abishag for making sure he was well, he was in shock. He had only a few words for him, let me put it in first person so that it sounds convincing that I was a fly on the wall when they were having this conversation. He said "Please let this be the last time I pick up after you, I cleaned up after your first mess so I will not clean up after this one instead I will clean you if you don't clean after yourself, it is not a threat but a promise". Ombogo was discharged from hospital and admitted to a private rehab that no one knows for him to get back on his feet, so Abishag did not have the pleasure of saying good bye or know how he was doing.

Some people are very observant, they take interest in what they do or what is around them. I think most successful people are able to make good judgement, take calculated risks and curve their lives the way they want their lives to be. This doesn't mean that divine intervention is not always in their favour most of the time but God gives you what you can handle. Then there are those who have photographic memory, I have had such friends they make life interesting for those of us who have selective amnesia. They remember dates, times, what was said what by who and why. Omera was one of those people who had a good eye for detail, especially where Abishag was concerned and I am not sure if it was love anymore or an obsession as he knew how Abishag's brain worked and how she deals with situations. Anyway when Abishag came back she was obviously grateful for what he had done for Ombogo but a bit disappointed that he went far beyond what he was supposed to do by making Ombogo disappear. Not that she wanted to see him but she wanted to be at least involved, in what and why, I don't know and I am not one to speculate.

When Abishag arrived at Omera's he was waiting for her with open arms and he seemed to be in an annoyingly good mood but Abishag was on the other end of the spectrum. Because she wears her heart on her sleeves, Omera knew that something had upset her. He knew better than to even ask how she found herself calling him in the middle of the night to come over as she was full of surprises "not sure" let's just say she was interesting that's why Omera was chuffed to bits by her. She landed in his arm and let out a sigh of relief as if she had been rescued by Zoro it was like a scene from the Wild wide west movies. She let go of her inhibitions and it was a night to remember am sure the fire brigade were on stand by but thankfully the two of them managed to contain the fire.

What I can say is that Abishag saw the moon, the stars, the mountains and the rivers and finally peeped into heaven and came back as they had both brought their A game. I don't know what happened because I was not a spectator at the ring side for this match I can only write what I was told. Abishag had forgotten that she was planning to go back home on that day so she hadn't prepared for what happened later.

Chapter 30

There comes a time in life when your life is at full speed that it is physically and mentally impossible to turn to turn back. The amount of investment you have put in an issue is too much for you to think otherwise 'and I don't mean financial' money is vanity as it comes and goes. Sometimes it is almost impossible to turn back you know like when the plane has gained height and is at cruising level, it is normally a point of no return because it is at cruising level, there is no way the pilot can just change his mind and decide he wants to take a break and land as they will either crash land. As for Omera, he had reached a Point of No Return, a place of do or die therefore he said a prayer as it was a day to hit the bullseye and get a game shot.

On that day Abishag had gone out for dinner with her village mate Omera supposedly went to play golf then headed home. What I don't know in the story is whether he went to play golf or watch Afro cinema from a distance. Omera was besotted with Abishag that he could sense when he was being brushed off or it was just a time to herself she needed. He had made it his mission to study and try to understand this woman who had made him lose focus of everything around him to put it simply. When he thought about this woman, he would smile to himself and think that is the woman he wouldn't mind seeing her face every morning when he woke up for the rest of his life. He had already pictured her with him somewhere exotic and sunny with grandchildren and a dog. He knew he was going to be benched and he was not one to be caught on his back foot. He knew he had to take interest in his competition and see what he was up against.

He already knew where Abishag would and would not go so this gave him an upper hand and was hopeful for the night and lucky enough he did. He went into a private booth and had a few drinks with a few people he met while using the corner of his eye seeing drama unfolding. Abishag's date was going on and on and Abishag seemed to be getting frustrated by the conversation and some point she had gone to the ladies and came back with a fresh face which is a never a good sign it is usually to calm down. That was Omera's queue to leave the restaurant discreetly and punching the air knowing he did not have to worry about his rival because he seemed to have shot himself in the foot. He went home a happy man and knew tonight his stars had aligned and if only Abishag could call him he would have been the happiest man alive because he knew her calendar (menstrual cycle) like the back of his hand.

When Omera received Abishag's call that night, he was ecstatic he knew and understood the assignment which was to make Abishag fall in love with him like never before and leave a lasting impression. He knew Abishag would be so consumed with what was going on around her that she was not thinking straight. Some would wonder if this was preying on someone else's vulnerability or marking his territory the only way he knew best.

So that Sunday morning Abishag woke up smiling and seemed to have no care in the world. She had been served breakfast in bed and not the Kenyan breakfast that consists of tea and bread but a full English cooked breakfast including all the fry ups. Did he want her not to get out of the bedroom and realise what could have just happened or not happened, was this a pull wool over someone's eyes? But Abishag was too happy to realise. The day was spent with them going out for dinner and then went back to "their home". Reality hit when Abishag had had time at work to reminisce over the goings on of the weekend as she had the epiphany of what went on during the weekend. She thought about going to the nearest chemist but then again it was up to 36 hours. She thought about it but then again think about it whatever will be will be, after all people like Lauren Silverman and Simon Cowell survived it and it worked about for them so why not. Anyway she hoped against all odds that nothing like that happened but if it did, she would cross that bridge when she reached it. On the other hand Omera was negotiating with God, promising to never look at another woman in that way if he granted him that wish.

Chapter 31

Could it be true that when someone has been disappointed so many times in relationships they tend to go for what they cannot get; to put it in a simplistic way and the reason behind it is because they know they are going to fail so they set themselves up for failure. But then again was is it safer that way just in case it does not work they have no regrets because they knew they were going to fail anyway?

I am just speculating on this one today or more of asking questions than answering any because I am trying to understand where we are going with this story wondering if Abishag playing a game or she in love with Omera; is she in this relationship because she knows she can't have him so this is a form of self-preservation. For example people tend to go to restaurants that are full and queue for hours for food that the next restaurant is offering they may not necessarily be serving cheaper or better food but because others are going to them we also just follow suit.

Abishag seems intelligent and although things did not go her way she had managed to pull herself together and achieve so much within a short period of time. At this time I think she was either using Omera to climb up the social ladder or she sees Omera as a lifelong partner. As she continued talking I was thinking, is she looking for someone to pay for the way she was treated before or her wounds have healed. Why did Abishag decide not to go to the chemist that Monday morning or even Sunday? Is she as innocent as she seems in this whole soap opera.

As days turned to weeks Omera was holding himself back not to ask her if she was alright or feeling unwell and summoned all the energy within him not to ask. Abishag on the other hand was relishing being in limbo as she didn't want to find out whether or not it was possible and had decided whatever will be will be and she was hoping that it would turn out positive for her to have a little man running around the house and her family would be complete, with or without a partner she was fine. Her parents had also expressed the desire to have more grandchildren and they could only achieve this through her because she was an only child as they say you love your children but fall in love with your grandchildren. Abishag was not worried about the outcome and she decided to go with the flow. Omera on the other hand was very curious to know if what he had planned worker and how he would cut down on his working hours and be a good father, he had accumulated enough wealth for him to take a step back and let other people run his business. He was so ready to have another child and he was hoping for a boy.

Weeks turned into months and Abishag was not giving away anything and she continued to work even more and she had no time for dinners or sleep overs. She was always busy until one day when she was in a very intense meeting, being grilled about a business hitch she got so worked up unknowingly and after the meeting, she rushed to another meeting so she excused herself because her colleagues wanted to stay behind for a less formal meeting. When she tried to stand up, she felt so light headed and went to reach for the table and she couldn't remember what happened after that and she woke up in the hospital with a drip in her hand and felt so embarrassed but thankfully her colleague had stayed with her the whole time. She asked what happened and she was told she fainted and was brought to the hospital by her colleagues and that is the time the penny dropped, she had a bun in the oven and she didn't want her colleagues to start asking questions because she was not showing instead she told the colleague that she was okay and would call her other friend to come and be with her because she knew she was going to be there a while.

The colleagues left when the doctor came into the room to speak with her, he asked her how hard she had been working, when was the last time she took a break from work and her fluid intake and then he finally asked the most important question, when the lining of her uterus was last released. I think sometimes we as humans we don't want to know what we know or what we need to know so that we cheat our brains into believing that everything is alright. We blame it on the weather, stress etc but when someone else confirms it and reality sinks in, it is not an interesting place to be, and at this point Abishag did not have an answer for the doctor. So he decided to carry out a blood test to confirm everything at once and she would know exactly how far gone she would be.

After an hour the results can back positive of pregnancy and the rest was fine but she was twelve weeks pregnant. The doctor suggested an overnight stay in the hospital and one week off from work. Abishag called her aunty to pick up her daughter from school for her. When she hang up the phone, guess who showed up at the hospital, Omera. Who told him that she was admitted in hospital? I guess we will never know. The drama continues tomorrow God willing. Have a fabulous day.

ABISHAG'S STORY

Chapter 32

There is a saying in Abishag's Maragoli village *"Hu wisingii tumiraho mba"* loosely translated as 'don't let yourself dry where you showered from'. It sounds better in your own mother tongue and if yours is English let's just go with the flow. As I am from the same tribe as Abishag, I asked my auntie to make me understand and this is what she said: That when guests come to your house let them wake up, shower but not shave their beard in your house, I still get confused up to now.

Anyway, that was what was ringing in Abishag's head when she Omera arrived at the hospital because she did not want anything else to do with him, the shower had been taken and it was time to go and dry herself from somewhere else as the fun was over and reality had sunk in and she didn't want to be the one held responsible for messing his life. It could be argued that it was already messed but at the same time there was no evidence at the time, now that there was tangible evidence of what was going on, she knew she was going to be blamed for trapping him. As usual when it all goes wrong it is always the woman who is blamed even when the man swore that his wife was either dead or they were staying together for the sake of the mortgage and children

Omera knew he was not going to get a coherent answer from Abishag on that day. In his heart he knew he had to up his game to win her over again and this time round there was no throwing money at it attitude because she would not buy it. He really wanted to have the woman but he knew it was going to be a sacrifice and something was going to give and this time round he knew it was up to him to make things work. When he asked Abishag what happened she said she felt faint because she has been too busy working and was not having enough to eat and no sleep. She also said she had been feeling unwell and she thinks she was coming down with malaria and he knew she was lying. They say a man knows when his weapon of mass distraction has discharged and caused havoc in some uncharted territory. So he knew there was no way of extracting that information from the woman and force was not going to work he decided to take the velvet glove approach. He asked if there anything she needed and of course she said she had everything. Omera left and said he would see her the following day and she said she would be at home and he knew her house was out of bounds for him. He knew it was time to regroup with himself and rethink on the best approach.

Abishag was discharged from hospital and went home to rest for the one week she was told to rest and was not going to let anything interfere with her wellbeing and Omera junior aka Sibuor. For some reason, she was so happy and content that she felt her life fulfilled which came as a surprise to her. She didn't feel any resentment towards Omera but love for him and thankful for meeting him but on the other hand she was not going to take that responsibility of him making the right choice or the next move and she couldn't wait to tell her girl about the news. I feel this was a good move to help the child understand what was happening and prepare her because life was going to change. Sometimes we as African parents don't tell our children anything, we forget that children have their own brains, they are human beings in their own right and have their own voice. Let us try and involve them especially where they will be affected in one way or the other or what we are going to do will have a significant impact on their lives. They can also help us as parents understand their world and how it works. In other words "Listen to the voice of a child" , sorry I digressed.

Later that evening when Abishag was resting she heard a knock on her door, it was Omera with the watchman with a lot of shopping on the other side of the door. She asked herself how he got into their compound as it was a private gated community. In my head I am thinking with that kind of car he was driving, she should have known the gateman or the watchman or security man at your gate would open saying "hello boss, karibu/akwaaba/ edupe/obulunji sebo/saobona/olibwanji" and there would be a bribe involved, this is Kenya we are talking about. There was no way he would be grilled at the gate by security.

Anyway he was in already and as a pastor's daughter you don't shut doors on people's faces. He was welcomed and her baby girl was excited to see a visitor with so much shopping. His excuse was he was just passing by in her neck of the woods and decided to pass by hers to make sure she was okay and had enough food to eat because she had said she wasn't eating much. He had brought T-bone meat for them to make good soup for the invalid with Lucozade as it is tradition in her community, he said nothing but just wanted to know how baby girl was doing at school and if she was happy and was there for one hour and left. Abishag looked at the shopping and knew she was not going to shop for the rest of the month.

Chapter 33

o not take a bath with your clothes on" This is the advice on old woman once gave to Abishag because she thought she was just getting the whole life thing wrong. When you are already in the bathroom, please just take off your clothes and shower properly. Whether it is a guest house, a hotel, or your neighbours house, you are already in the bathroom, there is no point you having your clothes and claiming you are having a bath, people know you are having a bath so why do it with your clothes on as it is all or nothing. Let us go back and talk about this morning sickness, cravings in pregnancy then you will understand where I am coming from.

Abishag like other women, had her own cravings that were draining her finances because it was a rear kind of seafood. In Kenya we know, sea food is not cheap as we have beef, chicken and goat meat but sea food is almost hard to get as it only found at the coast for the rest of the country we are grateful for the fresh water fish like Tilapia. The first and only time Abishag had sea food was during one of her crazy weekends with Omera and now the craving, she used to buy and just eat bit by bit not every time but as days went by, she felt the need to eat more of it. She was not ready to share these cravings with Omera because she could afford it but at this time she needed was to swallow her pride and ask for help.

Omera on the other hand realised that she was avoiding him like the plague although she would call him every day and talk about nothing. She was exceptionally sweet in her conversation and Omera knew that it was on purpose to keep him nice and sweet so he had to say something. He told her he wanted to meet her for dinner because she needed someone to speak to about a burning issue, she jumped at the idea for him being vulnerable and wanted to talk to someone as it felt so good to be needed. When they met, he aired out his feelings and that he felt so alone with no one to talk to because his girlfriend did not want him to have a role to play in his child's life and this shocked Abishag. She almost jumped to her defence ship and say she was not pregnant. He just looked at her and said he knew that she was expecting their child and that he was not naïve not to know that she was expecting. He knew what was going on and he was not happy that she didn't trust him enough to let him have a role to play in the whole pregnancy. He wanted to bond with his unborn child and the rest of the family to make it easier for him to continue bonding with them.

Abishag felt so guilty and with the raging hormones and everything else going on, she let out a flood of tears saying everything and Omera was shocked. She said the way she felt like she needs to smell him every time, speak with him and yet she was not able to because she was not sure of what she wanted any more as she thought about him every time which could be tantamount to emotional stalking. He just held her and waited for her to let it all out because it seemed like it had built up for a very long time. He just wondered why anyone would be in a bath with their clothes on, you will be wet anyway, you are better off going all the way, you will enjoy it better as the Maragoli would say "Kigwa Odore" the English would say "Finder Keepers". When you find something take it and use it well with no hesitation.

ABISHAG'S STORY

Chapter 34

It gets very confusing when a woman dates or marries an indecisive man and this is not to say that some women do not find it attractive but I think most often than not most women prefer a man who can take charge of a situation and by a man being indecisive he achieves the paradoxical effect of making him seem weak.

Don't get me wrong this does not mean that women want someone to completely take over their lives, no, it just means that they want some sense of security both physically and emotionally. Can you imagine if a woman is pregnant or stressed and gets a man who cannot take charge and her hormones are all over the place, what happens. There are strong women out there, powerful, regularly opinionated and totally self-sufficient, which is totally intriguing but they still need a man to take charge of some aspects of the relationship.

I think most men do not like a 'yes' woman or a woman who hangs on to their every word, they need someone who can hold an intelligent conversation 'not literally' and be mentally challenging, not annoyingly argumentative whatever that means. On the other hand these women still need a man who can take charge of solving problems and make them feel secure. Years of experience in relationships have led women not to want to take the lead in romantic relationships as this might seem overbearing. I know feminists might argue otherwise but am not one so I cannot make an argument on their behalf. The funniest line I hear mostly is 'It's up to you babes, or what would you like it to be' that's a man being indecisive and avoiding his responsibility. Let me explain why I gave you this long preamble.

Abishag and Omera were both strong minded individuals and both had their set ways, Omera knew that Abishag was not going to be taken in by his power and influence to jump in a whim. She was a woman who knew what she wanted from life although things do not necessarily go her way everytime, she tried so hard and be her own person. Omera had to gather all his inner masculine strength and bring out his alpha male persona for this relationship to go anywhere. He could opt to take a back seat and let nature take its own course but sometimes when you opt to wait for

Mother Nature you would be shocked that it may not go your way. As Swahilis would say "Chelewa chelewa utakuta mwana si wako" directly translated as keep delaying you will find the child is not yours. He knew it was time for him to strike before the child comes forth. He knew he had to do something to shape his destiny and not leave it to chance. Abishag on the other hand knew that this was a make or break time, to see how far Omera wanted to take their relationship. Was he the total man she needed or a man who didn't know what they wanted and was half in and half out or gambling with their relationship, anyway he decided to take a back seat and see what happens.

Abishag had many advisers telling her to fight for what was hers and decide for the man because men generally don't know what they want and they need a nudge in the right direction but she was not ready to do it because she didn't understand what that phrase meant. First of all, she could only defend what was hers and why fight in this case, she was not married to Omera so she could not claim him as hers. I can say I don't blame her, as a hopeless romantic she believed in love conquering it all and not fighting therefore she relaxed and decided to go with the flow but stand her ground not to relent to pressure of making do of what she had because of her circumstance. Baby no baby she was not going to turn into that woman who decides to move in with the man because she has his child. It hadn't worked before for her previously, what would make this situation different?

Omera knew what he wanted, he was at a stage in life where his happiness mattered and not what society would think. He was feeling sorry for his *"baby mama"* because she lived on the fourth floor in some nice apartments but the stairs were too much. He wanted her to move with him into his apartment that was closer to town, bigger and he wouldn't mind having a family living with him. He absolutely adored the little girl because there was something about her or was it just because he loved the mother? Although he also had an apartment it was on the 2nd floor and there was a lift in that flat therefore he tried his luck by telling Abishag that he was ready for her to move in with him. Abishag politely declined as she found it disrespectful and as she saw this as moving into a "shag pad", a house married men rent out to carry out their sexual endeavours often shared among friends.

Chapter 35

In all relationships there is always one reason to leave and a million reasons to stay or a million reasons to stay and one reason to leave depending on what you are gaining from it. This also depends on how you look at situations and what you think are important to you but you also have to balance risk versus protective factors a life is not black and white it is always about proportionality, this is what Abishag learnt this the hard way.

Her response to Omera had to be proportionate to what she had invested or gained in her relationship with him. She had to decide whether she would stay with Omera knowing he was still married and was never going to divorce his wife or the other option was to stay away and co parent with him and in extreme cases just disappear into oblivion and raise the child alone without "baby daddy" issues.

I tried to understand Abishag's point of view so she explained to me that one day she was at work and her workmates asked her who the father of her unborn child was and what got to her was not the question but the words that were used "who is the baby daddy". I do not think there is a woman who likes to be asked that question, it is easier if one is married or in a committed public relationship because it will be like asking an answer instead of a question, whether they are responsible for that pregnancy or not, it's the woman's secret.

Abishag felt like she had been stabbed by these words and because she couldn't name the person she just laughed it off as he is obviously a public figure and was very difficult for her because Omera's name is not the Kind you just throw out there in a conversation. The relationship police would translate it as her being a gold digger, a chancer or a home wrecker therefore this got her thinking, how the logistics would to work. She knew Omera was still married whether it was complicated or not that was the fact. On the other hand he was not offering anything substantial apart from finances and moving her into his apartment. Matters were made worse as Abishag went for every clinic alone, one day the midwife asked her who her birthing partner was, the only answer she had was I haven't thought about it. It was also tricky for Omera being in the public eye and anyway most women go for the clinics alone men usually don't understand why they need to be there.

Abishag had to have to think about what was going to happen there before the baby arrived. It was good being showered with shopping and sea food but unfortunately, Omera never ended up paying her rent and this made her remember when she was told "If he ain't paying rent, jump before you are pushed, he is part timing and not planning to stay", my understanding is he moved them into this expensive place but ended up not paying her rent, she paid herself. She knew she had to prepare herself psychologically to be a second time single mum and she knew it was easier when she had her first child although her relationship was rocky she had someone but now she was not sure what she had. This time round she was older and society would judge her harshly. When one is young they term it as young and foolish, while older ones are seen as failures who could not manage to domesticate/tame a wild cat. She was getting confused and asking herself if keeping the baby was the best move.

On the other hand Omera was busier than ever, he was away most of the time out of the country. He kept in touch constantly you know the Skype and FaceTime, viber, emo what is emo? But when he came back he went straight to his home to relax and catch up with what was happening while he was away. Abishag felt so alone like being alone in a crowd and questioned herself if she wrong not to move into the new apartment? She wanted more from him, she only knew his friends so she could not count herself as part of his family. He was not forthcoming with what the plan was, he did not show any signs of commitment. That apartment did not feel like a family home for her, it was good for an odd one or two weekends, it was like living in a hotel room, never feels like home.

Chapter 36

We all have that one knicker that has seen as through the years as it fits perfectly it is neither a thong nor a g-string, not seamless but if feels comfortable and doesn't show when you wearing any outfit. Most would like to call it a safe pair of knickers. For knickers enthusiasts like me you know you may have more than 50 pairs but there is always that one that you are always drawn to because it has seen you through lovely moments to the heart breaking ones.

So Omera had the same problem, he has that safe pair called his wife and on the other hand he had the thong or g-string called Abishag. His wife was like the Bridgit Jones ones, the one who holds you in proper places, makes you look beautiful in that dinner dress because it covers so much of your excess bits when you appear for a formal dinner you look very beautiful but when you are on a romantic escapade, you leave those one alone.

On the other hand Abishag was like a thong or g-string when you wear it makes you feel like you have conquered the world. It makes you feel confident and super sexy inside. You walk around smiling all day when you think of it so long as you buy a good fitting and not the cheap ones that you will spend the whole day moving it around because of discomfort. Although these kind of knickers are good and they make you feel like you are invincible in the world of lingerie, they are also not a day to day part of your regalia. They are worn when you need to add some extra oomph to your day. "Anyone below thirty, please disregard that statement because you can manage them everyday" but as you get older, it about comfort not looks.

Omera wanted to have the best of both worlds as we have noted above it is all about comfort the sexiness bit is done once in a while and not every time. I am sure that after dating most people let their guard down and opt to stay with their Bridgit Jones and this this may have been the reason Omera was disappearing. All this time Abishag thought Omera had been away, but he was in the country but he had had a surprise visit from the lady of the manor – his wife and they decided to go to Zanzibar with her for a romantic break. There were no work commitments anywhere he just couldn't trust that Abishag could handle being told that his wife had come to Kenya. He did not know how Abishag would react and that was not a chance he was willing to take because of his love for her and condition therefore he crossed his fingers and toes and hoped she would not find out.

As I had correctly guessed previously, he had his family home at some upmarket place in Nairobi therefore he moved Abishag to the current apartment so that he could rest assured that she would not go there for any reason because those are places you just don't go if you have no reason to and the chances of him bumping into her was next to none. The battle been won and it was time for him to rally back his troops and celebrate having conquered his latest conquest and just sit back and relax and wait for nature to take its course. After all men like him have no problem getting someone else young and vibrant, he is rich and easy on the eye.

ABISHAG'S STORY

Chapter 37

A man's heart plans his way, But the LORD directs his steps as the good book tells us. This is good because God always knows what is good for us at a certain time in our lives though we may not know at the time. The worst bit is when one decides to plan things and include another human being in their plans. Is it just me who has tried to plan with people and nothing materialises so I plan things alone. Not to discourage anyone who works better in pairs because most people do "we will" thing I don't I say I will because I don't know what the other person is thinking.

One morning Abishag was woken up with a sharp pain in the back and she thought a hot bath would soothe her because that's what hot baths are for. She ran her bath and went in, the pain was too much to bear because it was followed by some seriously bad stomach cramps. She draped herself in her bathrobe and went back to bed to see if the pain would stop but the pain wasn't going anywhere. She called her house help and told her she was not well she needed to go to hospital, her house help called Abishag's aunty who takes care of her baby girl sometimes. Aunty made her way Abishags place and found her in pure agony and decided to take her to hospital because she knew the baby was coming although it was not her due date yet. On their way to hospital they tried calling Omera but he kept sending the "I am in a meeting" auto text. So Aunty stopped calling and decided Abishag was her baby and she would take care of her herself.

On reaching hospital, she was examined immediately by the midwife who concluded that the baby had to be delivered immediately and Abishag was in such pain that she had never experienced before. In true village girl style she started calling on all her relatives and ancestors to pray for her she was dying, it was all theatrics in the labour ward as the echoes of her screams and shouts can still be heard in that hospital up to today I guess. The funniest one is when she kept saying in her mother tongue "whatever I was looking for in men, I have found it, so am never looking at a man again in my life, she told the midwife that if she sees her there again, she would need a psyche evaluation for mental health assessment. Aunty dearest called her mum and dad and told them their 2nd grand child was on the way as expected, they had mixed feelings because they knew she wasn't due for a few more weeks but her mother said she was on her way to the city and would be there the following day.

As the labour pains intensified so were Abishag's screams, she had declined the epidural because she had heard some harrowing stories about how people were left paralysed from waist down after. *"Am yet to see one"* am not sure so I can't say I know anything about it. After a few hours finally, the announcement came "She is crowning" and before anyone would react, the baby gave out some ear piercing sound the hospital staff had ever heard. They all said in unison in Kiswahili, "we've got a musician here" It was a baby boy. Everyone was so happy although it was not what Abishag had planned, she always dreamt that during labour, Omera would be there holding her hand, sweating it out with her, using his white handkerchief to wipe her sweat telling it was okay and he was right there with her', just like in the movies. She had to snap out of her day dreaming and face the reality that she was in this alone.

The baby came out as Omera's miniature, a certified true copy of the original and as it is with all premature children, they all have to be in hospital for some time. The neonatologist checked him over and said although he was premature he had a good set of lungs so he was okay and would stay in hospital for observation but there was nothing to worry about at that moment. Up until this time Omera had not answered his phone and as it happens when a child is born, all the attention is given to the child and the rest is forgotten.

Chapter 38

After their stay in hospital, Abishag left without hearing a word from Omera, he did not respond to her aunty and therefore Abishag was only left with her pride and she decided not to call him again as the Swahihili's say, "Nguo ya kukopa haistiri matako" translated as borrowed clothes do not cover your buttocks – it leaves you exposed. He was like a borrowed man, he was not hers as he was married to someone else.

Abishag's family had arrived in the city therefore she did not feel as lonely as she had felt before, she was glad she had such understanding parents and they were happy for the new addition to their family. She was discharged from hospital and she decided to go with her parents in the village because there was so much help and support at home. She knew she would not be happy living in that apartment which she had hoped that she would live with Omera and their children.

When all was said and done, Abishag was still human with feelings, she missed the company of Omera although she had a support system around her. It dawned on her that it was going to be more complicated than she thought when her son was six weeks old and needed to be registered at the registrar's and there was also the traditional naming, christening and shaving of the hair.

Abishag was happy that she had been blessed with a son but on the other hand, she felt like her life was not going according to plan. She could not believe that Omera had disappeared out of her life and she had put so much trust in him, she was aware that he was not divorced but she thought he was serious about their relationship. She felt so conflicted in herself because she had sacrificed a lot to be with him, she was a Christian and she had gone against her values to be with him. It was easier for her without a child but now she felt that she had let everyone down and she would be seen as a home wrecker and a husband snatcher. This sent Abishag into depression again, she became so withdrawn and was contemplating ending it all as she knew better and was raised well.

As days went by, Abishag resigned from her work, gave up her city apartment and decided to live at home in the village with her parents, it was too much for her to stay in the city. This worried her parents so much because they had seen this before and it sent her to a dark place and she struggled to get back to her baseline so they decided it was best she stayed with them until she is able to resolve her issues.

Abishag's son was baptised at her local village church and names after her father, he was shaved by her grandmother as her parents would not do it because of tradition. Tradition dictates that the child is shaved, circumcised and baptised by his paternal family as that is where he belongs. This was particularly important as according to the Maragoli tradition, the paternal side of the family and that is where he will be buried, burial sites are very important to Maragolis. If you understand tradition, if you were unwed and die, you are buried in a banana plantation in unmarked grave and if you a boy, when you die, your paternal family are sort and then sent their for burial whether they took part in his upbringing or not so you can understand her predicament.

ABISHAG'S STORY

Chapter 39

After a year of Abishag leaving at home with her parents and supporting in their family business of farming, her parents suggested that she goes for therapy as she had remained a shell of what she used to be. She had become more quiet, lost confidence, lost a lot of weight and was always in and out of hospital for one illness or another. Doctors were not sure what was wrong with her because they knew she was not well but could not diagnose her with anything. Some doctors suggested that it was bad luck as there were physical signs of illness but they could not diagnose her with any illness.

Abishag struggled with these illnesses and thought may be it was postpartum illnesses. She lost her appetite and was dependent on pain medication and anti acids to relieve her pain. This was so worrying that her parents decided that she goes abroad for treatment. Abishag was reluctant as she was not ready to leave her children at home to seek treatment and she also saw it as a burden to her parents. All this was too much for Abishag until she had a breakdown that led to voluntary admission to a mental health hospital for treatment. This shocked her but she only stayed there for twenty eight days and she was discharged with medication and a referral to a psychologist for therapy. This shocked Abishag into accepting that she had a problem that she needed to address.

Abishag's admission became a not so private affair as she was admitted to one of the best hospitals in Kenya for treatment and one of the Psychiatrists there was Omera's friend as they had met before. He was really saddened by what happened and decided to let Omera know that his girlfriend was not well and he needed to see her but he only told him after she had been discharged and left the hospital. This shocked Omera as he thought Abishag was the strongest person he had ever met and would survive anything. So he decided to visit Abishag in the village as he did not have her current contact details. He called Abishag's aunty and informed her that he would be going to the village to see her. Abishag agreed for the visit to take place but requested for some time to get better so that she would be able to engage with him. In the mean time Abishag took her parents offer to seek professional help abroad and she chose to come to the United Kingdom where she had relatives who would support her.

The meeting between Abishag and Omera never happened as Abishag applied for a standard visitor visa for private medical treatment. She left all behind and made her way to United Kingdom, landed in London and that is how we met. She has permanent residence now and this will be a story for another day.

I know some of my readers do not like the preambles before every chapter but let me explain why I do this. I have to do that for the me to get some direction on the story otherwise I will be all over and wouldn't be able to land any point. I would be circumnavigating around the story like Vasco Da Gama the Portuguese explorer. Anyway now you know and for those who know the street lingo it is called "kujichocha". That's just an excuse, me being a Maragoli, you know very well we do not go straight to the point, we beat around the bush and by the time we get to the point, we don't even know what we are talking about most of the time. The worst one is when someone wants to tell you that someone has died, they will give you their life history, reminisce over the good times they shared and then when they say they didn't want to eat anymore you know the person died. Now you understand why I go around in circles, it has been engraved in me.

ABISHAG'S STORY